THE
NANCY DREW
FILES™

Case 69
RUNNING SCARED

CAROLYN KEENE

D1341053

New York   London   Toronto   Sydney   Tokyo   Singapore

An Archway paperback
first published in Great Britain
by Simon & Schuster Ltd in 1994
A Paramount Communications Company

Simon & Schuster Ltd
West Garden Place
Kendal Street
London W2 2AQ

Simon & Schuster of Australia Pty Ltd
Sydney

A CIP catalogue record for this book is
available from the British Library

ISBN 0-671-85145-4

Printed and bound in Great Britain by
HarperCollins*Manufacturing*, Glasgow

RUNNING SCARED

Chapter

One

Isn't this fantastic?" Bess Marvin asked, turning to her cousin George Fayne on the balcony of their hotel room. Four stories below, the streets of downtown Chicago were buzzing with activity, and Lake Michigan sparkled under a sunny spring sky. "I can't wait!"

"*You* can't wait?" George arched an eyebrow at her cousin. "I thought *I* was the one running in the marathon on Sunday."

Bess laughed. "Sure, but that's three days away," she said. "Three whole days to explore all the clubs, restaurants, and *stores* here. Chicago is definitely my idea of shoppers' heaven."

"Anywhere you are is shoppers' heaven," Nancy Drew teased, joining her two best friends on the balcony. "What do you say, George—are you ready to go check out the course?"

Nancy and Bess had come with George to Chicago to cheer her on in the Heartland Marathon. Thousands of other women runners would also be competing, including the best female marathoners in the world. The three teenagers had made the drive from their nearby hometown of River Heights a few days early so that George could familiarize herself with the marathon course.

Their hotel, the Woodville, was the headquarters for the marathon. George had been lucky to get a room when the hotel had had a cancellation.

"Um, you guys aren't thinking of running the whole twenty-six-mile marathon course this afternoon, are you?" Bess asked dubiously. She twisted a strand of her long blond hair around one finger as she followed George and Nancy back into their room. "That's at least twenty-five miles over my limit."

Nancy laughed. She knew that the only sports petite, curvy Bess truly enjoyed were shopping and dating. George, on the other hand, with her tall and athletic build, loved physical exercise.

"You're hopeless," George said, rolling her eyes at her cousin. "And there's no way I'd run the whole course right before the marathon." She tossed her clothes on the fold-out cot that had been set up next to the room's two beds, then changed into a red T-shirt and white running shorts.

"Tell you what," George said. "Why don't you

explore Chicago while Nancy and I run? We should be back in an hour or two."

"Sure, I could do that," Bess agreed, letting out an audible sigh of relief. "Of course, if you *want* me to join you . . ."

George shook her head. "Nancy and I will be fine on our own," she assured Bess, tying on a bandanna to keep her short, dark curls off her forehead. "I want to register first, though, if that's okay with you, Nan. The registration room is just downstairs, on the second floor."

"No problem," said Nancy, stretching her long, lean frame. She had changed into yellow shorts and an aqua top that brought out the blue of her eyes and showed off her reddish blond hair.

"I'll come, too, since it's on the way out," Bess offered brightly.

After leaving their room, the girls took the elevator down to the second floor. A stream of people passing through an open door near the elevators told them where to go even before they saw the sign marked Heartland Marathon Registration.

Inside, the room was crowded with runners, officials, coaches, and reporters. Everyone seemed to be talking at once. "This is so exciting!" George said as she, Nancy, and Bess looked around.

Tables had been set up around the room and labeled to divide the runners alphabetically. George, Nancy, and Bess went to the table marked D–G, and George gave her name to the woman sitting behind it.

"Here's race information, a map of the route, and your ID number," the woman said, handing George a manila envelope. "And here," she went on, reaching into a large carton behind her, "is your official Heartland Marathon T-shirt."

"Cool!" Bess exclaimed as George held up the shirt for her and Nancy to see. It was light blue, and on the front was a gold silhouette of a woman runner. On the back Heartland Marathon was spelled out in gold letters.

"Thanks," George told the woman behind the table. She opened the envelope and pulled out the paper with her number, 6592, printed on it.

"Have you run the Heartland before?" the woman asked George.

"First time," George replied.

"One of our sponsors has provided bicycles if you want to explore the course," the woman explained. "You can sign them out and cover the route in about three hours or so. It depends on what the traffic's like."

George caught Nancy's eye. "Let's do it!" Nancy said.

"Great!" George said. "We may not have time to cover the whole course today, but we'll get to cover quite a bit of it."

The woman pointed to the opposite side of the room. "You can get the bikes just past the registration table marked W–Z. They'll tell you where the course begins—it's not far from here."

"Even *I'm* getting excited, George," Bess said as the three girls crossed the room, "and I'm not even running in this—oops!"

4

Bess stumbled against Nancy as a young man backed into her. "Excuse me," he said in a deep, slightly accented voice. "I must look where I am going." He was about six feet tall and very lean, with blue eyes and a head of curly blond hair.

"You're totally excused," Bess answered, giving the man her warmest grin. "I'm Bess Marvin, by the way."

"It is a pleasure," said the man, smiling back. "I am Jake Haitinck. Are you a runner?"

Bess giggled, then said, "Me? No, but she is." She flicked a thumb at George. "This is my cousin George Fayne and my friend Nancy Drew."

"I am very pleased to meet you," Jake said, shaking hands with the girls.

"Where are you from, Jake?" Bess asked before the other girls could say anything.

"The Netherlands. I am with the International Federation of Racing."

"What do you do, exactly?" Bess inquired.

Nancy exchanged an amused look with George. She didn't think Bess was too interested in the International Federation of Racing, but she seemed *very* interested in Jake Haitinck.

"Well, yesterday I measured the course, to make sure it is the official length," Jake answered. "Today I rode the whole distance on a bicycle and saw that it was all clearly marked. Things like that. This is my first time in Chicago."

"Oh, really?" asked Bess. "Would you like to see a little of the city?"

Jake's eyes lit up. "That would be wonderful!

But can you spare the time?" He nodded toward the bicycle table, just ahead. "You were going to take bikes out, weren't you?"

"No," Bess said quickly. "That is, my friends are, but I happen to be free at the moment."

"Then I accept." Jake checked his watch. "I will meet you at the front entrance of the hotel in ten minutes, all right?"

"Perfect," Bess replied, flashing him another smile. "See you then."

As Jake walked away, George shook her head in amazement. "This is a *women's* marathon, and Bess has managed to find the only cute guy around."

Nancy laughed. "At least now we don't have to worry about her getting bored while we're biking!"

"Nancy! See the woman in lavender?" George asked, nodding her head in the direction of a runner.

George and Nancy were riding side by side on a road in Grant Park. They were almost at the halfway point of the marathon course.

Following George's look, Nancy saw a muscular woman with straight brown hair pulled back into a ponytail. She wore lavender running shorts and top and a matching lavender sweatband. Nancy marveled at the way her feet seemed to skim over the pavement.

"She looks good," Nancy commented. "Do you know who she is?"

"That's Renee Clark," George said in an excited whisper. "She's young, but she's on her way to the top. See how relaxed her arms are? No strain. No waste of energy. She has great form."

As Nancy pedaled by, she studied Renee Clark's face. Her expression was serious and intent, but there was no sign that she was laboring. She looked as if she could go on running all day.

"Hey, isn't that a TV crew in that van?" George asked, breaking into Nancy's thoughts.

Looking up the road, Nancy saw a van driving very slowly. A logo on the van's side read ICT, with the words International Cable Television underneath. Through an opening in the roof, a man had a video camera trained on a woman who was running about twenty yards in front of where Nancy, George, and Renee Clark were.

The woman being filmed was tall, with bright red hair, and she wore a black T-shirt and black shorts with silver trim. She carried a stopwatch in her right hand. Next to her, a middle-aged man in a gray sweatsuit rode a bike. He watched the runner carefully and now and then murmured to her.

"Who's that?" Nancy asked George. "She must be someone special, to rate her own TV crew."

George looked, and her brown eyes widened. "She's special, all right. That's Annette Lang, the number-one woman marathoner for the last five years. Black and silver are her trademark colors. She's awesome! I can't believe I'm actually going to be running with athletes like that!"

7

As Nancy and George caught up to Annette, they slowed their bikes to the runner's pace for a moment.

"I want to watch her from the front," George said, picking up some speed. "She's tall, like me. Maybe I can get some tips by watching her."

Nancy decided to drop back to where the van wouldn't block her view. She slowed down even more and gazed around at the park's trees and greenery, enjoying the beautiful day.

The sudden roar of a car engine startled Nancy. She looked up and saw a black, rust-splotched car speeding out of an intersecting road and heading right toward the van.

Nancy gasped as the van swung sharply away from the car, leaning dangerously on two wheels. She waited for the crash, but at the last second the car turned. Without slowing, it sped down the road on which Nancy was riding.

About fifteen yards ahead of her, Annette and the older man with her quickly stepped to the grassy edge of the drive. Nancy veered her bike closer to the side of the road.

With a sudden chill Nancy realized that the car had also steered to their side of the road—and now it was heading straight for Annette Lang!

Chapter
Two

HER HEART in her throat, Nancy pedaled as fast as she could toward Annette, who seemed frozen in place.

The car engine roared in Nancy's ears as she leaned out and got an arm around Annette. She lunged from her bicycle seat, carrying the runner away from the car's path. A moment later the two of them lay sprawled on the grass by the road, breathless. The car barreled past, just inches from where Nancy and Annette lay.

Nancy whirled her head around. She got only a glimpse before the car vanished, but it was enough to see that the car had no license plate and the windows were tinted.

"What was that maniac doing?" the gray-haired man asked. He was kneeling next to Annette, with his bicycle on the grass next to him. Up close, Nancy saw that he was short and compact, with bristling eyebrows. His light blue eyes were flashing with anger.

"Don't move," he warned Annette as she started to push herself up to a sitting position.

The runner shook her head. "I'm all right, Derek, really. Hardly even bruised." She got up, then brushed dirt and grass from her clothes and hair. A small crowd had gathered, and Nancy noticed Renee Clark among them.

"Thanks to you," the older man said, smiling at Nancy. "Are you all right?" When Nancy assured him that she was, he said, "This is Annette Lang, and I'm Derek Townsend, her trainer. You have fine reflexes, young lady."

Before Nancy could reply, George came rushing up. At the same time the ICT van, which had made a U-turn, screeched to a stop, and three men and a woman piled out.

"Nancy!" George exclaimed. She jumped from her bike, letting it clatter to the ground as she hurried to her friend's side. "That car . . . it looked like a deliberate hit-and-run!"

Nancy nodded grimly. "It seemed that way to me, too," she agreed, getting slowly to her feet.

Derek Townsend frowned. "Deliberate? I don't think— The authorities would have to—"

"Nancy *is* an authority," George insisted. "She happens to be a detective."

The trainer gave Nancy a look of interest. Feeling self-conscious, Nancy smiled and introduced herself and George. She took a step for-

10

ward to shake Townsend's hand, then winced at a twinge in her left knee.

"Take it easy," a man beside her said. "That knee might be wrenched."

A young man whose knit shirt bore the ICT logo had come over from the TV van and was leaning over Nancy. He was tall, with warm brown eyes, a muscular physique, and wavy light brown hair that had streaks of gold in it.

Nancy flexed her knee and gingerly pressed the area around it with her fingers. "I'm pretty sure it's just bruised."

"If you're sure," the young man said. He held out his hand with a smile. "I'm Kevin Davis."

"Kevin Davis!" George exclaimed before Nancy could introduce herself. "The decathlon champ? From the last Olympics?"

Kevin swung around to face George, and a broad smile spread across his handsome face. "I only took a silver at the Olympics," he told her. "Now I'm retired. What's your name?"

"George Fayne," she answered, returning his smile.

"You look like a runner to me," Kevin commented. "Are you here for the marathon?"

George nodded. "Uh-huh. How about you?"

Kevin gestured to the van. "I'm with ICT. I'm the commentator for their marathon coverage."

"Really? Sounds like fun," George replied. A slight blush colored her cheeks, and her eyes were shining. In fact, it looked as if George and Kevin had forgotten that anyone else was around.

Smiling, Nancy turned away from the two. A few feet away Derek Townsend was watching closely as Annette did some careful stretches. The runner looked up as another member of the TV crew, a young woman with short black hair, came up.

"Ms. Lang, would you mind talking about what just happened for the cameras?" the woman asked.

Annette looked taken aback, then gave the woman a smile. "Uh . . . no, of course not."

Derek Townsend frowned. "I don't think—"

"It's all right, Derek," Lang snapped.

The woman turned to Nancy. "We've got some great footage of you rescuing Annette. Could you give me your name? We'd like to interview you, too."

"Uh, no, thanks," Nancy said quickly. "I'd prefer to remain anonymous."

"Well, it's up to you," the woman said, and turned back to Annette.

"I have to interview Annette," Nancy heard Kevin say to George as the crew was setting up. "Maybe we could talk more later—at dinner?"

George's blush deepened, and she said, "I'd like that. Why don't you join us? My friends and me, I mean."

"Great!" Kevin said. "Where are you staying?"

George told him, and they agreed to meet in the lobby of the hotel at seven.

"Kevin!" A television crew member called from the van, where the camera was set up and Annette Lang stood by. "We're ready to roll."

"See you at seven," Kevin said, and headed toward where Annette was standing.

A sound man gave Kevin a hand mike and directed him to the van, on the grass by the road. Annette was already standing in front of the van's ICT logo, with a cameraman facing her, and Kevin took his place beside her.

"Rolling," said the cameraman. Nancy and George moved in closer to watch.

"I'm speaking with Annette Lang, the top woman distance runner, who's just had a serious brush with danger," Kevin said into the mike. "Annette, it appeared to us that someone tried to hit you with a car while you were running. How do you feel? Do you have any idea what it was about?"

"I'm fine, Kevin." Annette threw a dazzling smile at him and the camera. Nancy was impressed by the runner's poise and confidence after her narrow escape. "I can't be certain what this was about. But there are people on the professional running circuit who envy my success and would like me out of the way. If they can't do this by fair means, maybe they're willing to try foul."

Annette straightened her shoulders and faced the camera squarely. "But it won't work," she went on determinedly. "I'll continue to run, and I expect to win on Sunday."

"Have there been other incidents?" Kevin asked. "Do you suspect specific individuals?"

Annette shook her head. "I can't comment on that, Kevin. I'll be happy to talk at length after the Heartland Marathon. Then I hope you'll interview me as the winner—and still the champ!"

She flashed another smile at the camera, then turned to her trainer, who was standing nearby, looking unhappy. "Let's go, Derek," she called.

Derek ran a hand through his gray hair. "I really think we should report this to—"

"*Derek,*" Annette interrupted. "I am going to complete my run. Period. Now, let's get going." She ran off, leaving Derek staring glumly after her.

Kevin turned quickly and held his microphone under Derek Townsend's nose. "Any comments, Mr. Townsend?"

"I . . . no, nothing. Not right now." The trainer looked relieved when the camera stopped rolling and the crew began putting the equipment back in the van. Sighing, Townsend picked up his bicycle.

He was about to pedal off after Annette Lang but hesitated and then beckoned to Nancy. "Miss Drew, are you really a detective?"

Nancy left George, who was talking with Kevin Davis, and went over to the trainer. "Yes," she told him, "but I'm just here to give my friend moral support in the marathon on Sunday."

"I see." Mr. Townsend looked around to make sure that no one could overhear them. "Perhaps your being here is a stroke of luck. Could I consult you this evening?"

"What about?" Nancy asked.

The trainer leaned closer, and his voice dropped to a whisper. "I can rely on your discretion? Nothing of this must get out to the media."

Nancy's curiosity was aroused. "What's this all about, Mr. Townsend?" she asked again.

"Call me Derek," the trainer insisted. "The fact is that Annette has received some very nasty anonymous notes, threatening harm unless she withdraws from the marathon. We didn't take them seriously—until now. But in view of what just happened here, I've had a change of heart," the trainer went on. "I think someone wants to kill Annette!"

Chapter

Three

You HAVEN'T TOLD anyone else about these notes?" Nancy asked Derek Townsend.

The trainer shook his head. "As I say, we didn't take them seriously. Annette didn't want her training interrupted, and she didn't want security guards getting in her way. But this hit-and-run business . . . what should I do?"

"I'd like to look at the notes," Nancy said after thinking a moment. "Could I see them tonight? We're staying at the Woodville."

"So are we," Mr. Townsend told her, "like most of the top entrants. I'll drop them by your room tonight." Nancy gave him her room number, and with a wave the trainer rode away.

Looking radiant, George walked over to Nancy. "You don't mind, do you, Nan?" she asked. "About Kevin having dinner with us, I mean."

"Of course not," Nancy replied, grinning at George. "I mean, it's not every night we get to have dinner with a gorgeous sportscaster who's totally interested in one of my best friends."

"You really think he is?" George asked, blushing. "I mean, he's this famous athlete and TV guy, and I'm just— You really think so?"

"From the way he looked at you, definitely," Nancy assured George. "But listen, something else is going on, too. I may have a case to work on while we're here." She quickly told George of Derek Townsend's concern for Annette.

As George listened, her smile faded. "That's awful!"

"I'll know more after I look at those notes later," Nancy went on, picking up her bike. "But now we might as well check out a little more of this course."

When Nancy and George finally returned to their room at the Woodville, Bess was studying herself in the full-length mirror on the back of the bathroom door.

"What do you think?" she asked, spinning to show off the electric blue silk minidress she was wearing. Its price tag still hung from one sleeve.

"It looks fantastic," George said. "Don't tell me you already have a date with that guy we met in the registration room?"

Bess let out a sigh. "Not exactly. Jake has a

really busy schedule until the marathon is over," she explained. "We took a walk and talked awhile. Then he said he had to go, but maybe we'd see each other later. So I went shopping for a dress to celebrate in after the race. How was your ride? Did you check out the course?"

"We biked well over half of it. It's awesome," George said excitedly. "There are going to be a few tough areas, but I think I have a good shot at a new personal best. I'm shooting for three hours and fifty minutes." She peeled off her clothes and disappeared into the bathroom.

While George took a shower, Nancy told Bess about the attempted hit-and-run in the park and the threatening notes Annette Lang was receiving. "Annette's trainer is coming by with the notes tonight," she finished.

Bess flopped down on her bed. "Are you going to investigate it?"

"Maybe," Nancy replied. "We'll see after I talk to Annette's trainer. Oh, I almost forgot," she added. She shot a meaningful look at George, who was emerging from the bathroom in a towel. "George has a date who's having dinner with us."

Bess sat up straight. "A date? How could you almost forget something that important! Who is he, George? How did you meet? I want all the details!"

Bess listened intently while George told her the story. "He sounds great," Bess said when George was finished. "What are you going to wear?"

"I don't know," George said. "What do you think? I wish I'd brought more dressy things."

Bess got up from the bed, went to the closet, and surveyed the clothes they had unpacked earlier.

"How about that dress I brought?" Nancy suggested. She pointed to a cream-colored dress of soft, lightweight wool.

"You'd look gorgeous in that," Bess said, holding the dress up to George. "Kevin will love it!"

"There he is," George whispered nervously as she, Nancy, and Bess entered the lobby at seven that evening. "Here goes." She smoothed the creamy wool of her dress and started toward him.

Kevin Davis was sitting in a chair in a waiting area just beyond the reception desk. He was wearing a navy blazer, striped shirt, and jeans.

When he saw George, Kevin rose from his chair, his eyes sparkling with appreciation. "You look great, George!" he said.

George responded with a smile that lit up her face. "You've already met Nancy, and—"

"Actually I didn't get Nancy's name this afternoon," Kevin said with a laugh. "She preferred to be called 'Anonymous.'"

Nancy laughed, too. "It's good to see you again, Kevin. And this is Bess Marvin, George's cousin."

"It's my pleasure—" Bess broke off as someone spoke up behind her.

"Hello, Bess." Jake Haitinck stood there, wearing a leather jacket over a button-down white shirt and a pair of jeans.

Nancy was about to suggest that Jake join them

for dinner, but before she could, a petite young woman with lustrous black hair hurried over to him.

"Jake! I must talk to you!" the young woman said, her dark eyes flashing angrily.

Jake looked embarrassed. "Ah . . . yes, of course. Bess, meet Gina Giraldi. She's a runner from Italy. Gina, this is Bess . . ."

Gina shot Bess a furious glare and turned back to Jake. *"Now,"* she said, crossing her arms.

With an apologetic look at Bess, Jake followed Gina to a separate grouping of chairs.

There was an awkward silence. Then Kevin cleared his throat. "I don't know about you ladies, but I'm starved. Let's eat, shall we?"

They made their way across the carpeted area to the hotel restaurant, called the Great Fire. It was decorated with old-fashioned furniture, gaslight fixtures, and velvet drapes. The menus explained that the historical prints on the walls showed Chicago as it had looked before the famous fire that had destroyed the city, in 1871.

They ordered, and while they waited for their food, Nancy noticed Renee Clark. She was sitting with an older, dark-haired man and a woman in a smartly tailored suit.

"Who's with Renee Clark, do you know?" she asked Kevin. It occurred to her that Renee was someone who would benefit from Annette being forced out of the marathon.

Kevin followed Nancy's gaze. "The guy is her trainer, Charles Mellor," he replied. "The woman is Irene Neff, a public relations rep for TruForm running shoes. Renee has an endorsement contract with TruForm, and Irene is probably trying to psych her up for the race. A win for Renee would be a major coup for the company."

"I didn't realize running was such a big business," said Bess.

"Don't kid yourself," Kevin replied. "There's a lot of money involved here—a twenty-thousand-dollar first prize, plus a car, for the winner. That's just for starters. What with running being so popular, shoe companies hand out a lot for endorsements. Renee gets at least a hundred thousand a year from TruForm. Then there are commercial deals, or the chance of a career in TV sports announcing. Distance *is* big business, especially for the top few runners."

Nancy knew that Renee couldn't have been driving the car that had nearly run down Annette Lang—she had been on the course herself. But perhaps Charles Mellor or Irene Neff had been behind the wheel. Nancy made a mental note to keep her eye on all three.

Just then the waiter appeared with their orders —prime rib for Nancy and Kevin, grilled chicken breast for George, and roast duck for Bess— and Nancy forgot all about the threats to Annette.

While they ate, Kevin kept the girls laughing with stories about his job. Nancy didn't miss the looks he and George kept giving each other. There was no mistaking the signs: a romance was definitely brewing between the two.

Nancy was just scooping up the last of her mashed potatoes when a familiar, grating voice spoke up next to her.

"Well, well, if it isn't Nancy Drew! Is the great detective snooping into something suspicious at the Heartland Marathon?"

Standing there with a smirk on her face was Brenda Carlton. The petite, dark-haired girl was a reporter for *Today's Times,* a River Heights tabloid, but sometimes Nancy thought Brenda's greatest talent was for botching up Nancy's cases. Already Brenda's loud comment had caused several people to turn their way, including Renee Clark, Charles Mellor, and Irene Neff.

"I'm just here to root for George," Nancy said, keeping her tone light.

"Really?" Brenda looked suspicious. "Even though they didn't mention your name, I recognized you on TV, saving Annette Lang from getting run over. Your being here doesn't have anything to do with that, huh?"

Nancy shook her head. "Just a coincidence."

"Annette seems to think someone is out to get her," Brenda persisted. "There may be a story there. Did you get a good look at the car?"

"It happened pretty fast, and all I saw was a battered car with no plates. I can't be more specific than that. Sorry."

Brenda's gaze landed on Kevin for the first time, and her eyes widened in surprise. "Kevin Davis! How do you know these three?"

"We just met today," Kevin explained. "And you are . . . ?"

Brenda smiled smugly and said, "Brenda Carlton, with *Today's Times.* No doubt you've heard of it. We have an impeccable reputation."

"For printing the trashiest stories around, that

is," Bess murmured under her breath, rolling her eyes at George and Nancy.

Ignoring Bess's comment, Brenda asked Kevin, "Did *you* get a good look at the mystery car?"

"Sorry," Kevin said apologetically. "I was watching Annette. Everything else was a blur."

An expression of annoyance flitted across Brenda's face. "I see. Well, I'd better be going, but I'm sure I'll be seeing you around." She walked to a table across the restaurant.

Kevin turned to Nancy, George, and Bess. "She seems a little full of herself," he said. Lowering his voice, he said to Nancy, *"Are* you planning to do any detective work here?"

Nancy hesitated before answering. "I don't know yet. But if it turns out that I am, I hope you'll keep it a secret between us. I work better when I can stay undercover. Which is why I didn't want to be interviewed this afternoon."

"You can count on me," Kevin assured her. "But your pal Brenda may have blown it for you. A lot of people heard her, and they'll spread the word."

Bess looked up from her salad and grimaced. "All this talk about Brenda is ruining my appetite. We need an antidote. I hear they have a rooftop dance club here that's pretty hot. Why not check it out after dinner?"

"Not me," George said. "Until the race I'm not staying up late."

"I'll go with you," Nancy told Bess. "I just want to stop at our room to see if Derek slipped those notes under the door."

Kevin turned to George. "It's still pretty early. How about taking a walk?" he suggested.

"Sure," George replied.

After the group paid the waiter, Kevin and George went out for their walk, and Nancy and Bess returned to their room, just across from the elevators on the fourth floor.

As she opened the door to their room, Nancy glanced at the floor. "No notes," she commented.

"I like Kevin," Bess said. "And I'm really happy for George." She closed the door behind them.

"Me, too," Nancy agreed. "I bet she won't even have to run Sunday's race—she'll be floating!"

Bess laughed, then broke off suddenly at the sounds of angry voices just outside their door.

"Are you threatening me?" a woman's voice demanded.

Nancy's eyes widened in surprise. She was sure that that was the voice of Annette Lang! Exchanging a look of concern, Nancy and Bess tiptoed closer to the door.

"I make no threats, I tell the truth," a second woman replied harshly, in a heavy accent. "Once before you cost me a race, Annette, and I do not forget these things."

Bess clutched Nancy's arm. "I recognize that accent! It's Gina Giraldi," Bess whispered. "She's the one who grabbed Jake when he came over to talk to me in the lobby tonight. She's got a temper that—"

"Ssh!" Nancy whispered, holding up a hand as she put her ear to the door.

24

"Stay away from me," Annette was saying angrily. "I didn't—"

"I'll get you," Gina interrupted shrilly. "Some time, some place—when you do not expect it and there is no one to protect you—I will get my revenge."

Chapter

Four

THERE WAS SILENCE, and Bess turned to Nancy. "Do you think Gina had something to do with that car today?"

"Could be," Nancy said. "She's definitely mad at Annette. We need to find out why." She listened intently for a few more moments. "I don't hear anything. I think they're gone."

Nancy cautiously opened the door and looked outside. The corridor was empty.

"Gina sounds like someone who could get violent, if you ask me," Bess said as Nancy closed the door.

"I wish I knew more about her," Nancy said.

Just then a quiet knock sounded on the door, and Nancy opened it. It was Derek Townsend, holding a manila folder. "Here are the notes," he said, handing the folder to Nancy.

Nancy walked over to the room's desk and opened the folder, with Bess looking over her shoulder. There were three sheets of plain white paper, on which letters clipped from newspapers and magazines had been pasted. All the notes were threatening:

This race *will* be hazardous to your health!
You can run but you can't hide!
You're an endangered species!

Bess gasped as she read the notes. "Isn't Annette scared?" she asked Derek. "If it were me, I'd break a speed record running for cover!"

"Annette isn't like that," Townsend replied. "She doesn't scare easily, even when it might be in her best interest."

"One thing about these," said Nancy, her gaze still on the notes. "They were written by someone who's familiar with American slang and usage. So they probably weren't written by Gina Giraldi. Her command of English is good, but it sounds formal, stiff. Not like these notes."

The trainer stared at Nancy. "You suspect Gina? But why would she do something like this?"

"She was having an argument with Annette out in the hall a few minutes ago. We heard it through the door," Nancy told him. "Gina threatened to get even with Annette for something that happened between them. Do you have any idea what it is?"

Townsend pressed his lips together. "There's bad feeling between those two," he admitted. "Gina thinks Annette plotted to have her disqualified from the New York Marathon last year —that's one of the biggest on the circuit. And Annette has accused Gina of sabotaging a friend of hers in another race."

"Sabotage?" Nancy echoed. "How?"

The trainer held up his hands in a helpless gesture. "You'll have to ask Annette," he said. "Personally, I think Gina might well be capable of sabotage—or worse. She can be really vicious if she has reason."

"What makes you say that?" Nancy asked.

"I saw her attack a girl who she thought was making a play for Jake. It took two men to pull her away. She has a streak of—"

"Jake?" Bess interrupted. "Jake Haitinck? You mean, he's her boyfriend?"

"He was," Derek Townsend replied. "Jake broke up with her months ago, but Gina hasn't accepted it. As far as she's concerned, he's her property."

Bess sat down on a bed. "Wonderful," she said faintly.

"What's wonderful?" George asked, coming into the room. Seeing Derek Townsend, she said, "Oh, hello." Then she saw the notes on the desk, and her smile faded. "Were those sent to Annette?"

Nancy nodded. "Derek, when and how did Annette get these notes?"

"One of the notes was waiting for us when we checked in here two nights ago. It had been mailed from somewhere in Chicago the day before. Another was stuck into Annette's purse yesterday. The third was slid under her door this morning."

"I need to talk to Annette," said Nancy. "I know she wouldn't go to the police and didn't want guards, but she has to understand that the danger to her could be serious. In order to be any real help, I'll need some more information from her. Will she cooperate with us?"

Townsend sighed. "I'll speak with her. I hope she'll be reasonable, but she *is* headstrong. I'll let you know." He retrieved the folder, then left.

As soon as the trainer was gone, George jumped up, excited to be able to tell her friends what had happened with Kevin. "Kevin and I walked to the lakefront—it's really close. And we talked and talked . . . about running, and athletics in general. I mean, he was such a great athlete, but he's really modest about it. And he was interested in *me*, what I like to do, my family, everything . . ."

George's voice trailed off, and she looked sheepishly at her friends. "Sorry, I guess I'm babbling."

"It's a good thing, too," Bess said, grinning at her cousin. "Otherwise, we would have had to pump you for all this information."

Giving George a hug, Nancy added, "We're really happy for you. Sure you don't want to change your mind and celebrate with us at that club upstairs?"

"What?" George gave Nancy a dazed smile. "Oh, no, I've got to be up early. Kevin has a busy day of work, but we're going to work out together first thing, before he starts. There's a health club that marathon entrants can use right down the block.

"Oh, I almost forgot to tell you!" George went on excitedly. "Kevin got a message at the desk. The networks picked up his story on the car that almost hit Annette. They used his footage on their news shows, even his interview. It could be a big break for him."

As George went into the bathroom to wash before bed, Bess and Nancy applied their make-up. Nancy was grabbing her shoulder bag from her bed when the phone rang.

"Hello?" she said, picking up the receiver.

"This is Derek Townsend."

"Hi, Derek. This is Nancy."

The trainer's voice sounded strained and agitated as he said, "Could you come to Annette's room right now?"

"What's wrong?" Nancy asked him.

There was a slight pause before Derek said, "I—I'd rather you saw for yourself. Please, come right away, it's Room four-twenty-eight, just down the hall from you. Hurry."

"I'll be right there," Nancy assured him, then hung up. She turned to Bess and George, a grave look on her face. "That was Derek Townsend. Something's happened in Annette's room, but he wouldn't say what. He sounded all shaken up, though. I'd better get over there."

"I'll come along," Bess offered immediately.

"Me, too," George chimed in.

The three girls walked to the end of the corridor and knocked on the door marked 428. It was opened immediately by Derek Townsend, who motioned them inside.

Nancy drew her breath in sharply as her gaze swept over the large room. It was a shambles. Shirts and shorts had been torn in half and thrown every which way. Several black-and-silver running suits had been shredded. Running shoes had been cut apart and hung by their laces in the open closet. Two canvas athletic equipment bags had been savagely ripped.

Looking pale and nervous, Annette sat with Derek on the room's couch. "Look on the dresser," Derek Townsend said, breaking the silence that had fallen over the room.

Nancy got a sick feeling in the pit of her stomach when she saw what was on the dresser top. A long, thin-bladed knife had been stuck through a running shoe and a piece of paper.

As Nancy looked at the paper, she heard Bess gasp behind her. On it was a crude drawing in black marking pen of a skull and crossbones. Underneath was another message composed of pasted-on magazine letters:

Your time is running out!

Chapter

Five

"THIS IS AWFUL!" Bess said in a horrified whisper. George shook her head in silent disgust.

After taking one last look at the threatening note, Nancy went over to Annette. The runner stared straight ahead, her jaw muscles clenched.

"Annette, can we talk for a few minutes?" Nancy asked gently. Gesturing to her friends, she added, "You've already met my friend George, and this is Bess Marvin."

Annette nodded to Bess and George, who sat down on the edge of the bed. Looking at Nancy, she said, "Derek says you might be able to figure out what's going on here."

"Possibly," Nancy replied. "How long were you out of your room?"

"I haven't been in here since I changed clothes this afternoon." Annette gave Nancy a weak smile. "After you saved my life. I left at about six to go have dinner at Fritz's Steak House. Then I talked to reporters in the press room. Derek found me there and told me about his talk with you. Then we came up here—and found this."

Nancy caught the look of surprise Bess gave her. "You didn't come in here at all between six and now?" Nancy pressed Annette.

"No, I just told you," the runner answered.

Nancy stood up. "If I'm going to help you, I need your complete honesty."

"What are you talking about? I *am* leveling with you," said Annette.

Squarely facing Annette, Nancy said, "Bess and I heard you arguing with Gina Giraldi in the hall earlier this evening. What were you doing there, if not going to or coming from your room?"

Annette hesitated briefly before answering. "Oh, that. Gina and I don't get along, it's no secret. We ran against each other in Europe, and we argued even then. After dinner I wanted to go to my room to rest, but when I got on the elevator downstairs, Gina jumped in and started yelling the same old stuff. When I got off, she followed me."

Annette shrugged. "I got fed up and told her to leave me alone. We stood there yelling back and forth until another elevator came. It was going up, but I got in anyway, just to get away from her. That was that."

"What happened to Gina?" George asked.

"I have no idea. I just left her standing there."

"Then she could have gotten into your room," Bess suggested.

"I wouldn't put it past her," Derek agreed.

To Nancy's surprise, Annette shook her head. "I don't think so," she said. "Gina's crazy, but this isn't her style. If she wanted to hurt me, she'd do something that would really hurt—trip me or kick me in a pack of runners, where it would look like an accident. She wouldn't give any warning, either. She'd just act."

"Why was she yelling at you?" Nancy asked.

Annette sighed wearily, then explained. "She was disqualified from the New York Marathon last year. A runner claimed that Gina elbowed her so hard she bruised her ribs and couldn't continue. It turned out there was a witness, and Gina was disqualified and fined. The witness testified anonymously, and Gina got it into her head that it was me. It wasn't, but now she swears she'll get even."

Nancy nodded, then said, "Derek mentioned something about Gina sabotaging a friend of yours. Can you tell me about that?"

"It happened earlier this year, in South America," Annette said. "My friend Maria Carlisle had to drop out of a race because of severe pain in her foot. Someone had put a jagged piece of metal under the insole of her shoe, and the pressure of her foot made the edge come through and cut her. *That's* Gina's style," Annette said bitterly.

"You think Gina did it?" Bess wondered aloud.

"Yes, I do. She went around smirking and

dropping little hints when nobody else could hear. 'Too bad about your friend' and 'Better check *your* shoes out next time,'" Annette said, mimicking Gina's voice. "Stuff like that. Of course, nothing could be proved."

Bess moaned, and Annette stared at her. "What's the matter?"

"Bess met Jake Haitinck today," George answered for her cousin. "And tonight Gina gave her an ugly look when Jake was talking to her."

Annette nodded sympathetically. "I'd keep my distance, if I were you," she told Bess. "Poor Jake. Gina won't let him look at another girl."

"Can you think of anyone else who might have it in for you to the point where they'd do all this?" Nancy asked Annette. "There are the notes, the hit-and-run attempt, *and* ruining your things."

Annette shrugged. "I'm number one now, and everyone else wants what I've got. Some of the runners make a personal thing of it and say I'm stuck-up, stuff like that. I admit I'm not Miss Popularity, but nobody's ever done anything this terrible to me before. I have no idea who it is."

"When you were interviewed today, you gave the impression that you could name people if you wanted," Nancy persisted.

"Did I? Well, if I did, I was stretching the point a little." Annette gave Nancy a sly grin. "Give the public what they want, right?"

Annette didn't seem to be taking this very seriously, Nancy thought. "You might also push whoever is responsible for the threats into doing something more extreme," she warned. "I'd cool it on hints like that. Anyway, I'll look into the situation, but please keep it confidential. As far as the rest of the world is concerned, I'm just here to root for George."

"If Brenda hasn't ruined that already," George said quietly.

"Annette, if you don't want to bring the police in," Nancy continued, "that's all right—for now. But a time may come when we have to tell them what's going on."

"Wait a minute—" Annette seemed ready to argue.

"That's not negotiable," Nancy cut her off. "I know you have your priorities here, but your well-being is *my* priority. Do we have a deal?"

Annette looked quickly at Derek Townsend, then replied, "Okay. I guess you know what you're doing." She stood up. "Now, if you don't mind, I'd like to call it a night. It's been a rough day, and I still have to straighten up this room.

Nancy, George, and Bess said good night and went back to their own room.

"It sounds as if anyone could have gotten into Annette's room and done that damage," George commented as she got ready for bed. "Gina could have or Renee Clark or Irene Neff—"

"Irene Neff?" Bess cut in. "Why her?"

"She has a stake in Renee winning the Heartland Marathon," Nancy supplied. "If Renee wins, it's good for TruForm, and that means it's good for Irene. So it's possible that *she* could have broken into Annette's room."

Nancy went over to their own door, opened it, and examined the keyhole. "It doesn't look as if it would be hard—a file or credit card would do the trick."

"You ought to know, after all the locks you've picked on your cases," Bess put in. She glanced at her watch. "Not to change the subject or anything, but it's not even ten, Nan. There's still time to get in a little dancing."

"I'm with you," Nancy said. "Let's . . ." Her voice trailed off as the phone rang.

"Not again," Bess muttered as George picked up and said hello.

"Oh, hi, Kevin," George said, her face brightening. "What? . . . Really? . . . That's great!" Turning away from her friends, she whispered, "I'm glad I met you, too. . . . Okay, see you tomorrow morning. . . . Good night."

She hung up and turned back to Nancy and Bess, her eyes gleaming. "That was Kevin."

"Gee, I never would have guessed," Bess said, grinning.

George didn't even seem to notice her cousin's teasing. "His agent just called to say he's setting up a meeting with a network sports executive," she went on, "about announcing on 'Worldwide Sports.' That's the big time!"

"That's fantastic!" Bess exclaimed. "You must be good luck for Kevin!"

"That's what *he* told me," replied George, turning red. "There's more, too. He and Annette have worked out a deal for exclusive interviews about her trouble here and how she's resisted the pressure to drop out of the Heartland Marathon. That's two big breaks in one day, and it's all because of his story on Annette. Isn't it great?"

As Nancy listened, a very disturbing thought occurred to her. "That's really exciting," she murmured, hoping she sounded more enthusiastic than she felt. "It's a great chance for Kevin—and for Annette. She'll be getting a lot of publicity as well, won't she?"

"But she's already on top," Bess put in. "She's getting about as much coverage as she could, isn't she?"

"Hmm," Nancy said. She didn't like what she was thinking, but she couldn't ignore it.

Kevin Davis seemed like an ambitious sports announcer, and "Worldwide Sports" was the biggest sports show there was. Nancy had assumed it a coincidence that Kevin happened to be on the scene when Annette was nearly hit by that car in the park. Now she realized there was another possibility. Maybe Kevin himself had maneuvered the attacks against Annette in order to *create* the story that would help build up his career. And if that was true, George was falling in love with a criminal!

Chapter

Six

"NANCY, DID YOU HEAR a word I just said?"
Bess's voice brought Nancy back to reality.
Blinking, Nancy saw that her two friends were
both looking at her expectantly.

"Oh—sorry," Nancy mumbled.

Bess placed her hands on her hips and said, "I
was just saying, if we don't hurry, we'll never
make it to that club. Let's go!"

"Right," Nancy agreed, shaking herself. She
glanced at George, wondering if she should say
something about Kevin.

Maybe I'm just blowing this all out of propor-
tion, she thought. She decided to hold off until
she found out more about the sports announcer.

Still, she was preoccupied as she and Bess said

good night to George and took the elevator up to the fifteenth floor, the rooftop level, where the club was located.

"Mrs. O'Leary's Cow." Bess read the neon sign outside the club's doorway. A small plaque explained that it was named after the cow that was supposed to have started the Great Fire of 1871 by knocking over an oil lamp.

Through the doorway Nancy saw that the walls were patterned with cartoon cows in funky outfits and sunglasses, dancing and sitting at tables. "I'm going to like this place," she said, grinning, as they went inside and looked around.

On the walls of the club were flashing lights, and a purple neon stripe edged the high ceiling. The whole place was alive with dancers, moving to rock music being played by a band set up at the other end of the room. The café tables lining the walls were crowded with people.

Nancy noticed a few women wearing Heartland Marathon T-shirts, though no one she recognized. Like George, the serious contenders would be in training and in their rooms.

"This is fantastic!" Bess said, speaking loudly to make herself heard over the amplified band. "George is really missing out!"

Maybe it was just as well George wasn't there, Nancy reflected. She really needed to talk to Bess about Kevin. "Listen, there's something that's bothering—"

"Hi, Bess! Hi, Nancy!" Jake Haitinck stood before them. "Want to dance, Bess?"

Bess hesitated and looked at Nancy.

"Go ahead," Nancy urged. "We can talk later."

A moment after Bess went with Jake to the dance floor, a guy wearing a T-shirt that said Terminally Hip asked Nancy to dance.

She tried to get into the beat, but her mind kept going back to the situation with Kevin and George. When the song ended, she excused herself. She saw Jake and Bess sitting at a tiny table by the wall and went over to join them.

"I'm sorry for the way Gina acted today," Jake was telling Bess.

Giving Jake a brilliant smile, Bess said, "Don't worry about it. It wasn't your fault."

"Still, I feel bad about it," Jake said. "Gina isn't really so terrible. Her—how do you say it?" He ran a hand through his curly blond hair, trying to think of the words. "Her growl is worse than her bite, you know?"

"Well, I *hope* so," Bess said with a nervous laugh, "but I keep hearing stories about how she's done terrible things to people she didn't like."

Jake waved his hand dismissively. "It is only rumors."

Nancy looked at Jake with fresh interest. As a member of the International Federation of Racing, he might have information that could help her get to the bottom of the attacks on Annette. "Do you know Renee Clark?" Nancy asked him.

Jake tilted his chair back against the wall. "Renee? Sure. She is a sweet girl. And a very good runner. She will be the best one day."

"Sounds as if you like her," Nancy said.

"Everyone likes Renee. She doesn't have an enemy. There is only one thing wrong with her."

"What's that?" Bess asked.

"She doesn't have what you Americans call 'the killer instinct,'" Jake replied. "She lets up when she is ahead. She doesn't like to embarrass another runner. Once she lost a race she should have won because of that. Her trainer, Mellor, and the woman from TruForm are always after her not to do that ever again."

Nancy recalled what Kevin had said about there being big money in distance running. "I guess Renee Clark must be a gold mine for Irene Neff's company," she commented.

Jeff gave her a skeptical look. "She will be, once she starts winning. TruForm Shoes is taking a chance on the future with Renee. Irene Neff got them to sign her to a very big endorsement contract. If Renee doesn't start winning, it could cost Irene her job."

Nancy sat up straighter, and Bess leaned in, suddenly more interested.

"What's Irene like?" Nancy asked Jake.

"Very tough, that one. All business."

Bess had started tapping her foot to the music. Turning to Jake, she asked, "Ready for another dance?"

Jake hesitated. "One more," he decided. "Then I have to go to my room. I shouldn't really be here at all."

As they went back out on the floor, "Terminally Hip" appeared and asked Nancy for another dance. She smiled but said no. She just couldn't enjoy herself when she was worried about George.

When Bess and Jake returned to the table, Jake said good night and left.

"He sure is tough to pin down," Bess said, sighing. "I tried to make a date for tomorrow, but he just said he's got a lot to do for the race and he'll call if he has time. That guy really has marathon on the brain," she finished glumly.

Nancy couldn't help laughing. "The marathon *is* his job, Bess, but I hope he gets done early so you can spend some time with him." Leaning closer to Bess, she asked, "Can we talk where it's quieter?"

Bess's hand flew to her mouth. "I totally forgot about that problem you mentioned! Sorry, Nan." She stood up and gestured to a set of glass double doors on one wall. "It looks as if there's a terrace. Let's go out there."

The two girls went through the glass doors to an outdoor space with some tables and chairs. Some of the dancers were cooling off there. Nancy chose an empty table a little removed from the crowd.

"What's the matter?" Bess asked.

"This has to be just between you and me for now, all right? It's about George."

Bess's blue eyes widened. "A problem with George?"

"Not *with* George exactly. It's about Kevin." Quickly Nancy told Bess of her suspicions about Kevin. While she spoke, Bess twisted a strand of her long blond hair between her fingers.

"I see what you mean," she said slowly. "That *is* a problem."

Feeling relieved that Bess was there to share her worries with, Nancy asked, "So what do you think we should do? I mean, don't you think

43

George should know that Kevin is one of the suspects?"

"Definitely," Bess agreed. "The main thing to remember is that George is our friend. I'm sure she'll understand why you're suspicious of Kevin."

"I hope so," Nancy said, giving Bess a grateful smile. But deep down she wasn't so sure.

"I can't believe George actually got up at six o'clock to go work out with Kevin," Bess said the following morning as she and Nancy were finishing breakfast in the hotel's coffee shop. "You couldn't pay me to do that."

Nancy laughed and flipped over the check the waitress had left on their table. "It's eight-forty now," she said. "George's note said to meet her at the gym at nine. We'd better go."

Glancing toward the glass wall that separated the coffee shop from the hotel lobby, Nancy saw Renee Clark coming in from the street with Charles Mellor and Irene Neff. Irene had a grip on Renee's forearm and was talking very intently to her.

Quickly Nancy got up and left the money for their breakfast on the table. "Come on, Bess. You can pay me back later. There's Renee Clark and her entourage, and I want to talk to them. Follow my lead, okay? We're big fans of hers."

Bess grinned at Nancy. "Whatever you say." She followed as Nancy left the café and approached the trio.

"This is the biggest opportunity of your career," Irene Neff was saying in a low, gravelly voice that seemed to contradict her elegant suit and sleek blond hairdo. "We're a team. Charles and I will do all we can, but you—"

"You're Renee Clark, aren't you," Nancy asked in a breathless, gushy voice. "My friend and I think you're terrific! We hope you win on Sunday, and we'll be cheering for you."

Renee gave them a delighted smile, as though she still found it fun to talk to fans. "Thanks!"

Ignoring Irene Neff's annoyed look, Nancy asked, "How do you feel? You think you can get a personal best?"

"It's possible," Renee answered, "if the weather is right, and I get a fast start." She put down the nylon gym bag she held in one hand and gestured to her companions. "This is Charles Mellor, my trainer," she introduced, "and Irene Neff, who works for TruForm Shoes."

When Nancy and Bess introduced themselves, Charles Mellor gave them a polite nod and a murmur of greeting. He looked very fit, with a dark tan and dark hair.

Irene Neff ignored the girls completely. Placing a hand on Renee's shoulder, Ms. Neff said, "Remember what I told you." She turned on her heel and walked away.

Renee followed the older woman with her eyes for a moment before turning to Nancy and Bess. "Irene's not usually like that," she said apologetically. "She just has a lot on her mind.

"Hey!" she added, staring at Nancy more intently. "You're the one who saved Annette yesterday! I saw the whole thing."

"I was just in the right place at the right time," Nancy said, trying to play down the incident.

"Did I understand that you're a detective?" asked Charles Mellor, regarding Nancy with interest. "I couldn't help hearing that woman in the restaurant last night. . . . "

Thanks a lot, Brenda, Nancy thought. Aloud, she simply said, "That's right, I am."

"Sounds fascinating," Mellor commented. "Would it be asking too much to know what you're investigating right now?"

"Nothing, at the moment," Nancy told him. "We came here to see the marathon."

"Right," chimed in Bess. "And root for—"

"For *you,*" Nancy said quickly, flashing Renee a big smile.

"Well, I hope I can win it," Renee said. "I have to get going now, but it was nice talking to you. Charles, see you at the gym after my workout."

"Right," said Renee's trainer. After nodding to Nancy and Bess, he turned and ran to catch an elevator whose doors were just closing. Renee walked toward the doors leading to the outside.

"Brenda sure messed things up last night," Bess said to Nancy. "Who knows how many people know you're a detective now?"

"That's not going to make my job any easier," Nancy agreed. "Come on. I need to make a quick trip to the ladies' room, then let's go meet George. We're late."

A few minutes later the girls left the hotel. It was a crisp, clear day, and Nancy paused on the sidewalk to draw in a deep breath of spring-scented air.

"Have you decided what to say to George?" Bess asked.

"Not yet," Nancy admitted. "I have to talk to her today, though."

Bess nodded. "Good idea. She should know about Kevin before she gets too—"

Wham!

Nancy jumped back abruptly as a large object came hurtling by them from somewhere above and smashed into the sidewalk!

Chapter
Seven

INSTINCTIVELY, Nancy covered her face with her hands. Dirt and sharp fragments were flying everywhere.

After a few seconds the air was calm again, and Nancy dared to look up. "Bess! Are you okay?"

Bess nodded, her eyes wide with fright. Dirt and leaves speckled her jeans. "What happened?" she asked, looking at the object that had caused the crash.

A few feet in front of where they stood, the shattered fragments of a large ceramic planter lay scattered on the pavement, along with a plant and a pile of earth.

It had to have come from the hotel, Nancy

realized. Whirling around, she stared up at the windows. Her heartbeat quickened as she caught a glimpse of a head ducking inside. Quickly she counted the floors.

"Someone was looking out from the ninth floor," she told Bess, and dragged her back toward the hotel entrance. "Come on!"

A small crowd of people was hurrying over to them. "We're fine," Nancy said, pushing past everyone. She and Bess raced inside and went to the elevators. It seemed to take forever until one finally arrived and they were able to jump in.

By the time they reached the ninth floor, all the other passengers had gotten off. The doors slid open, and Nancy found herself standing face-to-face with Gina Giraldi! Gina gave them a cool glance and stepped inside as Nancy and Bess got out. The doors closed before they could speak to her.

Without pausing, Nancy started down the hallway to the right. "I'm pretty sure the room would have to be in this direction," she told Bess.

When they got to Room 926, Nancy paused. The door was ajar. Ready for anything, she pushed it wide open and went in.

A quick glance told her the person had gone. There were stacks of papers and manila folders on the room's low coffee table. The window was wide open, and when Nancy went to look down, she saw the remains of the planter were directly below.

"Gina was on this floor just now," Bess said, joining Nancy at the window. "She could have pushed that planter out." Her voice trembled as she added, "You don't think she did this because I talked with Jake last night, do you?"

"Maybe," Nancy said grimly. "Or maybe she doesn't want me looking into the attacks on Annette."

She turned around and leaned against the windowsill to think. "Maybe it wasn't Gina at all. Let's take a quick look around up here, then go down to the reception desk and find out which rooms our suspects are staying in. I'll bet one of them is in here."

After leaving Room 926, the two girls looked up and down the hallway but saw no one. Then they took the elevator back to the lobby and went to the front desk. When Nancy said that she was running the marathon and asked for the room numbers of her dear friends Gina Giraldi, Irene Neff, Charles Mellor, and Renee Clark, the young woman cheerfully supplied them.

"Bingo!" Nancy exclaimed after thanking the woman and walking away. "Nine twenty-six is Irene Neff's room! And she left us when we were in the lobby talking to Renee."

"But Gina's also on the ninth floor, in nine-fifteen," Bess put in excitedly. "I bet she got into Irene's room and tried to bean us with that planter. She's got the temper for it. And she was right there."

"That's true," Nancy said thoughtfully, "though it seems unlikely that she'd take the risk of sneaking into Irene's room. On the other hand, Charles Mellor and Renee Clark are even less likely candidates, since their rooms aren't on the ninth floor."

Bess's expression brightened. "There's one person who *definitely* couldn't have done it," she said. "Kevin. He's with George at the gym."

"You're right. But we have to consider the possibility that there's more than one person involved here, so Kevin still isn't off the hook."

Nancy's attention was distracted when she happened to glance at the nearby press room. There was Irene Neff, talking with Brenda Carlton, who had a portable cassette recorder in her lap.

"Well, well, there's our top suspect now," Nancy murmured. "Let's try to talk with her."

As they approached the doorway, Irene was saying, "TruForm makes the finest running shoes ever designed. We wanted the best endorsed by the best, and that's Renee. I'm certain that she's on her way to number one. Not just for one race, either—for all time."

"That's quite a claim," Brenda said. "What about Annette Lang? She's got to be one of the all-time best."

Irene lifted her shoulders in a slight shrug. "Annette's all right. She's had a good career, but now she's going downhill. Renee Clark is the future of distance racing. Ask anyone."

Brenda gave Irene Neff a sly look. "I understand you wanted Annette to endorse TruForm and that she turned you down."

This is news, Nancy thought, although she wasn't sure if it was the truth or a concoction of Brenda's, designed to get a juicy reaction.

"Where did you hear that nonsense?" Irene snapped. "Did Annette tell you that?"

"We journalists have to protect our sources," Brenda said smugly. "I'm not at liberty—"

"Never mind. It's not true. Actually, *Annette* wanted to sign with *us*, but we said no. Renee was the one I wanted."

Nancy had heard enough. "Sorry to interrupt," she said, entering the press room with Bess, "but I need to see Ms. Neff for a minute. It's important."

Brenda glared at Nancy and Bess. "How come you have to interfere with a reporter on the job? I thought *you* were only here on vacation."

"I'll be right back," Ms. Neff assured Brenda, sparing Nancy the need to reply.

The TruForm rep gave Nancy and Bess an appraising look, then followed them to some chairs that were out of hearing range of the press room. "Nancy Drew, right?" the woman said impatiently as she sat down. "Let's make this quick, whatever it is. I've got a million things to do today."

"We thought you should know that we were almost brained a few minutes ago by a large ceramic pot that fell from your room."

Irene Neff's mouth opened, but no sound came out of it. *"My* room?" she finally managed to say. "But that's— Are you certain?"

"We just came from there," Nancy told her. "The door was ajar, the window was wide open, and there wasn't a plant in sight. Did there used to be a large potted plant in your room?"

"Yes," Irene replied. "But when I left my room

before breakfast this morning, it was still there. I haven't been back since." Irene wrung her hands, and her eyes darted around. "You mean, someone else . . . ? I don't understand."

"When we met you with Renee Clark this morning, you walked away," Nancy pressed. "You didn't go to your room?"

Irene's hazel eyes narrowed. "What's with all the questions?" she demanded hotly. "What business is it of yours where I went? Look, I'm sorry about what happened, but I had nothing to do with it. Now I'm afraid you'll have to excuse me."

"One last thing," Nancy said as Irene started to walk toward the press room. "If you didn't push the planter out the window, that means someone got into your room. Any ideas on who it is or how they got in?"

"None," Ms. Neff said. She walked away without looking back.

"There's something funny about her," Bess said under her breath.

"She was definitely defensive," Nancy agreed. Then, glancing at her watch, she said, "Whoops, we're already half an hour late to meet George!"

The girls arrived at the nearby Pinnacle Club just a few minutes later. The front area was richly carpeted, with several couches and chairs. Posters of well-known athletes from Chicago's professional sports teams hung on the walls.

"Oh, yes," the blond young man at the desk said when Nancy supplied their names. "Your friend has already taken care of the guest fee. You'll find her through there."

Nancy and Bess were heading toward the gray metal door he indicated when George came through it, dressed in sweatpants and a T-shirt. Sweat-dampened curls stuck to her forehead.

"Kevin just arranged to tape an interview with Annette while she's using some of the exercise machines here," George said excitedly. "The club's giving him exclusive use of the big workout room for an hour. He's going to get some terrific material out of this!"

Nancy stepped aside as the door opened again. This time a group of runners walked out, grumbling among themselves. Gina Giraldi was with them, and she had a ferocious scowl on her face. The runners were obviously angry about having to cut short their workout because of Annette's interview.

Renee Clark was right behind Gina. She was the only one who didn't seem upset. She gave Nancy, Bess, and George a smile as she passed by. "My trainer was supposed to meet me here," Nancy heard her say to one of the runners in the group, "but since our workout ended early, I guess I'll just go back to the hotel and find him."

"Where's Kevin?" Bess asked, drawing Nancy's attention back to her friends.

"Oh, he had to make arrangements for the TV crew to come. He'll be back soon," said George.

Giving George a concerned look, Nancy asked, "When did he leave?"

"A while ago," George replied. "He had to cut his workout short when he got the idea of using the gym as background for the interview."

Nancy felt a rush of anxiety. So Kevin *could* have pushed that planter out the window. He was as much a suspect as ever. She would have to talk to George about this—and soon.

"Is Annette here?" Bess asked.

"She was supposed to be here by now, but I haven't seen her yet." Shrugging, George added, "Oh, well, I'm sure she'll be here in a few minutes. Hey, come take a look at the women's locker room. It's awesome! Steam room, sauna, whirlpool, lounge—you name it!"

She led Nancy and Bess through the gray metal door and past a huge room full of exercycles, stair climbers, weights, and some other equipment Nancy didn't recognize. At the far end was the door to the women's locker room. George pushed it open, and Nancy and Bess followed her in.

"Nice," Nancy said, looking around. The locker room was spacious, with wooden benches and shiny red lockers.

"And you haven't even seen the whirlpool and sauna yet." George grinned. "There's even a—"

"Ssh!" Nancy said suddenly. Cocking her head to one side, she strained to identify the faint noise that had caught her attention.

A thumping noise was coming from the far end of the locker room.

"What is that?" asked Bess.

"The whirlpool and sauna are back there," George said. She led her friends down an aisle of lockers and around a corner.

The thumping grew louder as they approached the sauna door. Then Nancy realized that the noise was actually coming from a door next to the sauna. She tried the door, but it wouldn't open.

"Hello?" she called. "Who's in there? Are you all right?"

There was silence.

Worry ate at Nancy as she reached into her shoulder bag and pulled out the lockpicking kit she always carried. She selected a slender length of flexible steel and inserted it into the keyhole. A moment later there was a click. With George and Bess looking on, she pulled the door open.

Nancy gasped as a body fell limply to the floor at her feet.

It was Annette Lang!

Chapter

Eight

O<small>H</small>, <small>NO</small>!" Bess exclaimed. "Is she . . . ?"

Nancy's heart was in her throat as she bent over Annette to check her pulse. Just then, Annette stirred, and the three teens let out a collective sigh of relief.

"I'll get help," said George, turning to go.

"No!" Annette's voice, urgent and harsh, stopped George in her tracks. "I don't need help. I'm all right. I just blacked out for a second. That closet was so small and dark. I've been afraid of places like that since I was a kid."

The runner struggled to rise, helped by Nancy and George. Bess grabbed a stool for Annette from in front of a locker. Breathing deeply,

57

Annette sat down. Her hair was a mess, and her clothes were disheveled, but she didn't seem to be hurt.

"Are you sure you're okay?" Nancy asked, kneeling by Annette's side. "What happened?"

"I'm fine," the runner replied. "I came in here a little while ago to put on my workout clothes. Everyone else was getting dressed to leave. Then, about a minute after everyone left, the lights went out. Someone grabbed me from behind, wrestled me into that closet, and locked the door on me."

"Did whoever it was say anything?"

Annette nodded. "I think it was, 'Get smart and drop out, lady, or next time you'll really get hurt.' It was something like that, anyway."

Nancy had to admire Annette; she didn't appear upset or frightened. It was probably just this grit and strength that had made her a champion.

"Could you tell if the person was a man or a woman?" Nancy asked.

"The voice was kind of a whisper, there was no way to know. Whoever it was was strong," Annette said. "It all happened so fast. . . . "

Nancy frowned. "Maybe you should have a guard until the race," she suggested.

"Look, I can't talk about that now," Annette said. "I've got the interview to get ready for, and I look horrible. Will you excuse me?"

Nancy looked at Bess and George, who just shrugged. "All right," Nancy agreed reluctantly. "We'll be right outside."

Annette went to a sink with a mirror over it and began to work on her hair. As Nancy,

George, and Bess left the room, Nancy saw that the light switches were just inside the locker room door. Anyone could have pushed the door open and flipped off the lights. With no windows the locker room would then be pitch-black.

"Gina Giraldi was here, did you notice?" George said, once they were back in the big exercise room. "Renee Clark, too."

"Renee couldn't have done it," Bess objected. "Everyone says she's so sweet and not competitive enough."

"The thing is, we can't eliminate anyone," Nancy pointed out. Including Kevin, she added silently. She decided that now was the time to talk about Kevin.

"George . . ." she began.

"Hi, there, ladies!" Kevin called, entering the exercise room with his crew. He pointed out a weight machine where he wanted them to set up, then came over to George, Nancy, and Bess.

"Is Annette here yet?" he asked.

When George told him what had happened to Annette, Kevin looked genuinely shocked. Then again, Nancy thought, part of his job was putting on a face for the camera. Maybe he was just acting.

Soon after, Annette appeared from the locker room, looking cheerful and refreshed. Kevin hurried over to the runner and grabbed her hands.

"Nancy told me what happened. Listen, are you sure you want to go through with this right now? I mean, we could postpone it."

"No, let's go ahead," Annette said with a

bright smile. "I'm fine, really. It was just a few minutes in a closet, after all."

"Okay, if you're sure," Kevin told her. "Actually, this is going to be a nice additional bit of drama for us."

Nancy caught Bess's eye and knew Bess was thinking the same thing she was: Maybe Kevin had had someone shove Annette into that closet. He might even have done it himself, to create that "nice additional bit of drama."

"I guess you'll be sticking around to make sure nobody drops a TV light on my head," Annette told Nancy blithely. Then she walked over and joined Kevin.

Nancy was steaming when she joined Bess and George behind the camera. As far as she was concerned, Annette's attitude stank. She wasn't taking this seriously enough at all.

As the interview began, Nancy noted that Annette seemed totally unaffected by what had just happened. She looked great and spoke easily and freely. After discussing her training routine, Kevin brought up the subject of the threats and assault attempts.

"Yes, there have been some threats and attacks on me in the last few days," Annette said, her expression growing serious. "But I won't let my life be controlled by the people who are responsible for this terrorism. I intend to run and win."

"She looks good," Bess whispered.

"Mmm," said George, but her eyes remained focused on Kevin.

When the interview was over, Kevin said, "Great! Now we'll shoot some cutaways."

"Cutaways?" Annette repeated.

"TV slang," Kevin explained with a smile. "We'll shoot you using a stair climber, exercise bike, and so on, without sound. Then we'll use those shots over the dialogue. Otherwise, it'd look too dull."

As they started to film the cutaways, Nancy leaned close to George and said, "Listen, we have to talk about Kevin. I think you should—"

"Can't it wait?" George cut in. "I want to shower now, so I'll have a few minutes with Kevin after this is done." George disappeared into the ladies' locker room before Nancy could reply.

Nancy sighed. Obviously her talk with George would have to wait until Kevin wasn't around. When George emerged from the women's locker room and rejoined Nancy and Bess twenty minutes later, filming was just ending.

"Okay, that's it," Kevin announced. "This is going to look great, Annette, and *you* look fantastic."

Seeing George, he went over to her. "I have to look at the tape and help edit it. If you want, you could watch us do the editing."

"Sure," George agreed. "I've already done my workout here, and I guess my training run can wait until this afternoon."

Kevin gave her a big smile. "Great! Let's see . . . it's eleven. Meet me in the hotel lobby at one, okay?"

George nodded. "Fine. See you then."

"Tell you what," Annette said, coming over to Nancy and her friends a second later. "I need to do some shopping, since all my gear was shredded last night. Do you want to come along?"

Nancy was surprised at the invitation but relieved that she wouldn't have to fight to accompany the runner.

Ten minutes later the foursome was back at the Woodville. They went over to the concierge's desk, and Annette said to the woman there, "We'd like the name of a good sporting goods store."

"Maybe I can help you out," said a gravelly female voice.

Nancy turned to find Irene Neff standing at a nearby message board, where notes were posted for marathon participants.

"Hello, Irene," Annette said coolly. "Know a good place to buy running gear? I suppose your opinions on *that* ought to be reliable."

"I know all the best stores, dear," Irene returned. "That's my job, to know the best—the best shoes, the best stores, the best runners."

Annette simply shrugged, but Nancy was aware of an intense current of hostility vibrating between the runner and Irene Neff.

"Try the Winning Margin," Irene suggested. "It's a new store in the Magnificent Mile district. You can get there quickly by cab, and the store has good-quality things."

"Thanks, Irene," said Annette. "If it's good, I imagine they'll have other brands than TruForm."

Annette turned to leave, but George held her back. "I just want to leave Kevin word about where we're going, in case we're late getting back." She scribbled a hasty note and left it on the message board, then followed the others out.

The Winning Margin was an enormous place full of every brand of sporting equipment and clothes.

"Hey, Bess, come with me while I look at running shoes," George said, pulling her cousin down an aisle toward the footwear area.

Bess grinned at Nancy over her shoulder. "Did you ever think you'd see the day when *George* had to drag *me* to go shopping?"

Nancy laughed, then followed Annette to a section where running clothes were displayed. "I'm surprised that you have to shop for this stuff at all," Nancy commented. "Don't you get free stuff from a lot of companies?"

"Sure," Annette told her, pulling an outfit in green and gold from the rack. "I market my own line, too. You saw those black-and-silver suits— those are my trademark colors. I'll wear one of my designs in the race on Sunday. But I still like to shop for other stuff I like."

Annette selected several items to try on. Naney decided to try on some tops and a yellow warmup suit with neon blue trim.

At one end of the department there was a hallway leading to a row of dressing rooms. Nancy didn't see a sales clerk, so she took her things to a booth while Annette went to another.

After sliding the curtain closed, Nancy hung her things on the hooks provided. She changed first into the yellow-and-blue outfit, then studied her reflection in the booth's full-length mirror.

The fit was perfect, Nancy noted with satisfaction, and the yellow fabric set off the rich reddish blond of her hair. She would definitely buy that one, she decided. She stepped back to grab the matching warmup jacket from another hanger.

Nancy had gotten her arms partway into the sleeves when suddenly someone behind her threw a sweater over her head and face. Then, before she could react, she felt herself being grabbed around the neck, also from behind!

She jerked her arms instinctively upward to dislodge the hands at her throat, but the half-on jacket blocked her movement. The powerful hands applied greater pressure, cutting off her windpipe. She opened her mouth to scream, but no sound came out.

Nancy started to feel faint. She couldn't see anything, and the ironclad grip around her throat continued to tighten. She was powerless to fight!

Chapter

Nine

THINK, DREW, Nancy ordered herself. She forced herself to ignore the pain and suffocating feeling that threatened to overwhelm her. Dropping her hands, she sagged back against her assailant, as though losing consciousness. The hands around her neck relaxed slightly.

That was all Nancy needed. She kicked back with her shoe, feeling a sharp impact as it connected with her opponent's shin. Summoning all her strength, Nancy spun out of the deadly grasp and stumbled forward, tearing at the sweater that was covering her face. She turned, but there was no one in the booth with her. She had to take several heaving breaths before she felt clear-headed enough to step out through the curtain and into the corridor between the booths.

It was empty.

"Annette!" she croaked. Her head ached, and her throat was sore and tender.

"What is it?" the runner called back.

Nancy swallowed to moisten her throat. "Someone just grabbed me through the curtain of my booth. I fought him off, and he ran."

"What! Hang on, let me get my clothes on."

A minute later Annette joined Nancy in the corridor. As she hastily zipped up her jacket, Annette asked, "Are you all right?"

"I'm okay, but it was a scary moment," Nancy said. She headed out to the sales floor. "I want to see if anyone noticed anything."

There was now a salesclerk on the floor. She was helping a woman choose a sweatsuit. "Excuse me," Nancy said to them. "Did anybody run out of this corridor just a minute ago?"

The clerk stared at her, and Nancy realized she was still wearing the running clothes she had been trying on. "Run out? Sorry, I didn't notice," the clerk said. "Why? Is something wrong?"

Nancy saw Annette shake her head slightly. "No, it's all right," Nancy said. "Um, I'll just go change out of these, then."

Nancy was conscious that the clerk was watching her as she and Annette walked back toward the dressing rooms. Nancy quickly changed back into her jeans skirt and white blouse.

"I was just thinking," said Annette. "Whoever did that obviously thought you were me."

"Maybe," Nancy agreed. "Or it was someone

who doesn't want me to investigate your case. The question is, who knew we were coming here?"

Annette scowled. "Irene Neff did, for one."

Before Nancy could comment, George and Bess walked up, both carrying plastic shopping bags. "I got some fantastic running shoes," George said.

"And I called Jake at the hotel. Lunch is on!" Bess added excitedly. "I found the best—" She broke off and stared at Nancy. "What's wrong?"

When Nancy explained what had happened, Bess's hand flew to her mouth, and George asked quickly, "You're all right?"

"Fine," Nancy assured her friends, "except for a bruise on my throat."

"Most of the suspects in this case spend all their time in the gym, Nan," Bess said. "They're *all* strong."

"But they didn't all know we'd be here," Nancy pointed out.

"Irene knew," said George.

Nancy nodded and thought, So did Kevin. You left him a note. And anyone could have seen that note—Gina or Renee, anyone at all.

"Well, shall we go back to the hotel?" Annette suggested. "I'd like to get something to eat, and I need to get in a run this afternoon."

Giving the runner a stern look, Nancy said, "I'll join you on that run. I don't think you should go out alone."

"I need a run, too," George said. "I have to meet Kevin at the hotel, but I can meet you later."

Annette shrugged. "Fine. I won't be running long or hard—not with the race two days away. I have to save most of my energy for Sunday."

"Yikes!" George gulped, looking at her watch. "It's almost one o'clock. I have to meet Kevin!"

At the hotel Bess raced up to the room to get ready for her lunch date, and George left for the ICT studio with Kevin. Nancy and Annette checked the message board, then went up to the runner's room. It was undisturbed.

"What now?" asked Annette, closing the door and looking irritated. "Do you plan to stay with me *all* the time? Is that necessary?"

Nancy crossed her arms over her chest. "I just wanted to make sure that your room was safe. You don't seem to understand that you may be in real danger." It wasn't easy making Annette grasp the seriousness of her situation.

"There are several people who stand to gain if you can't run Sunday," Nancy continued. "Renee Clark would be more likely to win, Irene Neff's company would get good publicity, Gina Giraldi would have her revenge. . . . And there may be others. You agreed to cooperate with me."

Annette gave Nancy an apologetic smile. "Sorry, I'm not used to having a bodyguard around. Okay, I'll behave. And I won't go anywhere until we run later this afternoon, all right?"

"Fine," said Nancy, smiling back. "I'll meet you in the lobby at three, then."

Nancy left Annette's room and went down the hall to her room, where she looked up the address of TruForm's Chicago office. It was only a short distance away. Nancy walked to the office, hoping that Irene would be out on business or having a late lunch.

TruForm occupied a suite of offices that were decorated with modern furniture. Nancy asked for Irene Neff and was directed to a corner office. When she got there, a secretary was just putting on her jacket in an outer room.

"Hi," Nancy said brightly. "Irene here?"

"Not at the moment," the secretary told her. "Can I help?"

"But she said she'd be here," Nancy lied, trying to look disappointed.

The secretary shrugged. "She's out of the office for the afternoon, and I'm going to lunch."

Perfect! Nancy thought. Aloud, she said, "I'll try another time, then." Before the secretary could ask her name, Nancy walked away.

She paused at a water fountain just down the hall, then bent to take a drink. She watched from the corner of her eye as the secretary picked up her shoulder bag and passed behind her. The woman didn't even seem to notice Nancy.

Nancy looked up and down the hall. Then she returned to Irene's office and tried the door. To her relief, it swung open. Nancy slipped inside and closed the door behind her.

The office was bright and attractive, with huge windows and modern chrome and steel furniture. Posters from TruForm advertisements hung on the walls. A big advertisement featuring Renee Clark hung behind the desk.

There was a filing cabinet in one corner, and

Nancy went over, opened the top drawer, and flipped through the files. They seemed to be arranged alphabetically, yet Nancy failed to find Renee's folder among the Cs.

Frowning, she moved to the next drawer, where the Ls were. There she found a folder labeled Lang, Annette, and she pulled it out.

A copy of a letter from Irene to Annette was the only thing that caught her eye. In the letter TruForm made a large endorsement offer to the runner. So, Irene had been lying when she said that TruForm had turned down Annette's offer of endorsement!

Of course, Nancy could understand why Irene wouldn't want to admit publicly that TruForm had been turned down by a top runner—it would be bad public relations. Nancy knew she needed better proof than this, though, if she was going to prove Irene was behind the threats.

After replacing the file, Nancy went over to Irene's desk. Her pulse quickened as she spotted a folder with Renee Clark's name on it. Nancy leafed through the contents.

"Mmm. Interesting," she murmured, pulling out a letter. It was addressed to Irene and signed by the chief executive of TruForm Shoes. The letter was dated just two weeks earlier.

The tone of the letter was friendly enough, but the substance was serious: It had been Irene who had gotten the company to gamble big money on the future of Renee Clark, the chief executive stated. Renee's future had better start *now*. If the deal with Renee didn't begin to pay publicity dividends immediately, the letter went on, Irene would find herself out of a job.

Nancy let out a whistle as she restored the letter to the file. In the race for a prime suspect, Irene Neff had become the front runner.

Finding nothing further of interest, Nancy slipped from Irene's office. Luckily, most of the other offices' occupants seemed to be out to lunch. Nancy's growling stomach reminded her that she needed to eat, too. After shooting a smile at the receptionist, she breezed out the office door.

She had a quick lunch of pizza and soda, then returned to the Woodville. She had twenty minutes before she was due to meet Annette and George. Time enough to go up to the room, change clothes, and think about the case. Nancy took the elevator to her floor, then stood in the empty hall, fishing through her purse for the room key.

Just as she found it, a loud angry voice erupted from somewhere nearby. With a shock Nancy realized that the voice was coming from *her* room. It didn't sound like Bess or George, though. She ran the few steps to the closed door.

Her key was in the lock when a terrified scream rang out from inside. This time Nancy recognized the voice. It belonged to Bess!

Chapter

Ten

Nancy flung open the door and rushed inside.

Bess was backed up against the wall next to her bed, her face white as chalk and her eyes wide with fear. Gina Giraldi was standing in front of her. Her face was a mask of rage, and her hands were clenched into fists at her sides.

"Nancy, help!" Bess cried. "She's insane!"

"Leave him alone!" Gina shrieked.

Nancy ran over and quickly stepped between the two girls. "That's enough, Gina," she said. "You're asking for trouble. Now get out of here."

The dark-haired runner spun around to face Nancy. "Aha, the lady detective speaks," she sneered. "What I promise, I will do. Your friend will suffer if she does not do as I tell her."

Nancy took a step toward Gina. "If you do anything to Bess, it'll be the dumbest move you ever made. If we have to call the police, you're out of the marathon."

Gina's sneer remained in place, but she left without a word. As Nancy closed the door, Bess flopped facedown on the bed.

"Are you all right?" Nancy asked.

Bess rolled over onto her back and looked at Nancy. "I'm fine. I was just afraid, that's all. She's the scariest woman I've ever met."

Nancy sat on Bess's bed and put a comforting hand on Bess's arm. "She was threatening you about Jake, wasn't she?"

Bess nodded. "The thing is," she said, sitting up on the bed, "I've already decided he's not my type."

"Not your type?" Nancy gave Bess a puzzled look. "How come?"

"It was our lunch date that did it. All he's interested in is running. He talked about how he likes being with the runners' federation, how he used to run, how great he feels working with runners, blah, blah, blah. I tried to change the subject, ask him what kind of music he liked, or what kind of stores they had in the Netherlands, but he'd just start talking about running again."

Nancy couldn't help laughing. "Sounds like you made the right decision," she said. "I'm sure Gina will lay off you now."

"I sure hope so," said Bess. She lay back down

on the bed and stared up at the ceiling while Nancy changed into sweatpants and an Emerson College T-shirt that her boyfriend, Ned Nickerson, had given her.

"When are you going to talk to George about Kevin?" Bess asked.

"This afternoon," Nancy answered, sighing. "I can't put it off any longer."

Nancy entered the lobby, wheeling the bike she had gotten from the second-floor marathon room. Seeing no sign of Annette or George, she went over to the message board, but there wasn't any message for her there.

Renee Clark was also there, with her trainer and Irene Neff. Nancy had just greeted them when a familiar voice spoke up behind her.

"Hi, Nancy! How's your *vacation* going?"

Wearing a triumphant grin, Brenda Carlton walked over to Nancy.

"Hello, Brenda," said Nancy, stifling a groan. "Get any hot stories lately?"

"Actually, I'm on the trail of something major," Brenda said smugly. "I'm meeting Gina Giraldi later, and she's going to give me the lowdown about who's doing dirty deals."

Pointing a manicured nail at Nancy, she continued, "And I bet I find out who's behind the attacks on Annette before you do. What's that I see in your eyes, a little jealousy?"

Nancy felt like strangling Brenda. Renee, Charles Mellor, and Irene Neff were eagerly drinking in every word Brenda said. Not only that, but Kevin and George had come up while Brenda was talking, and Kevin was listening. Now practically every suspect in her case knew that she was looking into the attacks on Annette!

Speaking through gritted teeth, Nancy said, "Can I see you in private?" Without waiting for an answer, she pulled the reporter away from the group by the message board.

"Hey, cut it out!" Brenda protested. "You're hurting my arm!"

Nancy let go, once they were far enough away to talk without being overheard. "Don't you have any sense?" she snapped before she could stop herself. "You just broadcast it to everyone in the lobby that Gina could make trouble for people. What if Gina is planning to finger one of them? You might have put her in serious danger!"

"You're just worried that I'm going to show you up for the overrated fake you are," Brenda purred. "Sorry, Nancy, but I'm keeping on this story. You'll just have to read about who threatened Annette in *Today's Times.*"

Brenda strutted off, leaving Nancy simmering.

As Nancy rejoined the others, Annette appeared, wearing silver-and-black running shorts and a matching top. "Ready?" she asked Nancy and George.

"George just has to change," said Nancy with a nod toward where Kevin and George were holding hands and talking quietly together.

Tapping her foot impatiently, Annette called, "George, can we get going?"

George looked up, slightly taken aback. "Oh—

sorry. I'll only be a minute," she said. After saying goodbye to Kevin and arranging to meet him after the run, she hurried to the elevators.

"Sorry I can't go with you," Derek, Annette's trainer, told the runner, "but I have to meet with that fellow upstairs in the marathon office. Where are you going to run?"

"In Grant Park, south along Lake Shore Drive," Annette said. "If that's all right with you," she added to Nancy.

Nancy ignored the slight touch of sarcasm in the runner's voice. "Sounds fine," she said.

"Have fun," Kevin told Nancy and Annette. "Well, I'd better go. I'm already late filing the piece I just edited." He waved and headed for the hotel's entrance.

"I'm off, too," Derek added.

After he left, Nancy and Annette drifted over to scan the message board while they waited for George. There were dozens of memos, appointments, questions, and answers. Nancy's eye was caught by an unusual piece of stationery with a red marbled design. Written on it, in a distinctive backhanded scrawl, was "Grant Park, 3:30. Fountain."

Nancy looked up as George reappeared, wearing a cutoff pair of orange sweatpants and a blue T-shirt. "Sorry I kept you waiting," she told Annette. "And thanks for letting me run with you. You don't know what a thrill this is for me!"

"Relax your arms!" Annette told George. "Your fists are clenched, and you're wasting energy. It makes your whole body more tense."

Annette and George were running side by side through the park, with Nancy pedaling alongside. Annette had been giving George pointers as they ran, and George looked as if she were walking on air. Even if Nancy was on a dangerous case, she was glad that it gave George the opportunity to train with the best.

The weather was cool, and there was a slight breeze. Somehow, in the park, the noises and crowds of the city seemed a lot farther away than they actually were.

"You're right," George told Annette after taking several strides. "I can feel the difference already. Thanks."

Nancy smiled at George, but a sober thought kept nagging at her. Every time she had tried to talk to George about Kevin, she had been interrupted by something. It was hard getting George away from Kevin long enough to tell her, but now she would do it. If only she could—

Zing! A high-pitched whining distracted Nancy from her thoughts. A split second later a piece of bark flew from a tree just alongside her.

Huh? Nancy thought. What was—

She jumped as a puff of dust kicked up just in front of Annette.

With a flash of panic Nancy realized what was causing the disturbances: bullets.

Someone was shooting at them—and using a silencer!

Chapter

Eleven

"**A**NNETTE! GEORGE!**" Nancy shouted, stopping her bike with a jerk. "Somebody's shooting at us. Head for cover!"

The other two didn't wait or ask questions but raced for the side of the path.

Her heart pounding, Nancy jumped from the bike and threw herself to the ground on the other side of the path from George and Annette. She was fairly sure this was the side the shots had come from.

With a quick turn of her head, Nancy saw that the other two had taken shelter behind the thick trunks of two old oaks. "Are you guys all right?"

"Fine!" George yelled back.

"I'm okay, too," Annette added.

"I'm going to look around!" Nancy shouted to them. "Stay put until I get back."

"Should you do that?" Annette called. But Nancy was already on the move.

She darted from tree to tree, heading away from the path and up a rise. The sniper would probably choose high ground, she reasoned.

Even though she was behind a tree, Nancy felt exposed and defenseless. She fought back her fear and forced herself to look ahead for a clue to the shooter's position.

Nancy froze as a bullet whined by, chipping the tree just above her head. In the next instant she saw a flash from a thick tangle of bushes.

Racing from tree to tree, Nancy headed toward the bushes where she had seen movement. She was about fifty yards away when a figure in dark clothes and a ski mask bolted from the brush and ran, away from Nancy.

Nancy took off in pursuit. "Stop!" she yelled, but it was useless. The person reached a road that was at a right angle to Lake Shore Drive. He leapt into the driver's side of a light blue car with a big scrape on the right rear fender. The engine roared to life, and the car screamed away as Nancy reached the road.

Breathing deeply, Nancy tried to squelch her frustration. She hadn't gotten a good look at the person at all!

Just before the car disappeared out of sight, however, she noticed something that made her start. The car had an ICT placard in the side window!

"Uh-oh," Nancy said out loud. She hadn't

actually identified Kevin, but there were no two ways about it—she had to talk to George *now*.

Nancy's mood was grim as she walked back to where the sniper had hidden. She spotted a gleam of metal in the bushes, bent down, and picked up an empty bullet cartridge. A fast search uncovered two more, which she pocketed. Then she hurried back to the spot where Annette and George were still pressed against the tree trunks.

"All clear," she announced. "Whoever it was got away."

George's face was pale as she emerged from behind her tree. Annette also seemed a little shaken.

"Hey, look at that!" Nancy exclaimed as her gaze lit on a huge structure nearby.

"That's Buckingham Fountain," Annette said.

Water was pouring down the sides of the multitiered fountain to a pool that surrounded it. Something stirred in the back of Nancy's memory, but she couldn't bring it into focus.

"Did you see the person?" George asked, breaking into Nancy's thoughts.

Nancy braced herself. George wasn't going to like what she had to say. "No, whoever it was wore a mask," she began. "The person jumped in a car and escaped." She took a deep breath before adding, "I did notice one thing. The getaway car had a placard with the ICT logo in the window."

George stared blankly at Nancy for a moment. "ICT? But you don't . . . you *can't* think that Kevin is involved with any of this!"

Nancy took another deep breath. "I hope not. But look at what this story is doing for his career. He could have caused any of the incidents. And now, the ICT placard in that car . . . I have to look at the facts, George."

Nancy saw a brief flash of pain in her friend's eyes. Then George looked down and tugged at the cutoff hem of her sweats. "He just would never do any of those things, Nancy," she said, still looking down. "You have to believe that."

"I want to, George," Nancy said quickly. "But until I know for sure, I have to consider him a suspect."

Finally George met Nancy's gaze. There was a determined glint in her eyes as she said, "Well, fine. I mean, I guess I understand. But *I* already know for sure, and I'm definitely going to keep spending time with him while we're here."

George walked away, kicking some gravel on the path, then leaned down and ran one hand through the water in the pool.

Nancy followed George with her eyes for a moment, then forced herself to deal with the case. Turning to Annette, she said, "Now that you've been shot at, we have to call in the police."

"But you said you wouldn't! I trusted you!" Annette cried angrily.

"I said I'd try not to. But now you've been shot at, and that's where the police come in. Otherwise, we're all in deep trouble."

"But what if they won't let me run?" Annette demanded.

"You'll have to work it out with them," Nancy replied. "Now, you and George wait here while I find a phone."

Nancy trudged up the road. Great, she thought. George is upset, and Annette won't let herself be protected. So much for my fun weekend in Chicago!

Fifteen minutes later a police car drove up to the spot where Nancy had found a phone. Two plainclothes police officers got out.

"Are you Nancy Drew?" asked one officer, a thickset man with jet black hair and long sideburns.

When Nancy nodded, he said, "I'm Sergeant Lew Stokes, and this is my partner, Detective Matt Zandt. Where are the other girls?"

"Waiting for us, back where it happened," Nancy told him. "I'll take you there. In the meantime you'd better take these," Nancy said, pulling the three spent cartridges from her pocket and handing them to the sergeant.

As they drove to the site of the shooting, Nancy told the officers about the other threats and the attempted hit-and-run, as well as about Annette's being locked in the health club closet and her own experience at the Winning Margin.

As she went on, she was aware that Sergeant Stokes was scowling. "We saw that thing with the car on TV," he said at last, "but the rest is all news to us. Just what do you think you're playing at here?"

"We had hoped to clear everything up without a lot of publicity—" Nancy began.

"You amateurs make me sick!" Detective Zandt exploded, speaking for the first time. He was a tall man with a red face and thick, brushed-back blond hair. "People get hurt because of people like you."

There was no point in arguing, Nancy decided, especially since she had been saying basically the same thing to Annette a few minutes earlier.

At her direction the officers parked the car and made their way down to the path where Annette and George waited. The two police officers questioned the three girls about all of the threats and attacks. When Nancy mentioned Kevin as one of her suspects, George opened her mouth as if to object. Then she clamped it shut again and turned away.

At last the questioning was over, and the officers drove the three girls back to the hotel, with Nancy's bicycle loaded into the trunk. No one said anything, and Nancy found her mind wandering.

Suddenly an image of the fountain in the park flashed into Nancy's mind. "The fountain!" she said excitedly. "Buckingham Fountain!"

"Nancy, have you lost your mind?" George asked. "What are you talking about?"

Nancy whirled to face Annette. "There was a message on the board in the hotel lobby today that said, 'Grant Park. Three-thirty. Fountain.' Did you notice it?"

Annette's eyes flitted nervously. "A message? There were a hundred messages on that board. Why would I notice that one?" The runner's cool self-control seemed to be cracking a little—not that Nancy could blame her. She *had* just been shot at.

"We were shot at in Grant Park, at three-thirty, by the Buckingham Fountain," Nancy explained, leaning forward excitedly. "That note was to tell the sniper where we'd be. But who else knew?"

From the front seat Sergeant Stokes asked, "Any chance that the note is still on the board?"

"We'll be at the hotel in a few minutes," his partner spoke up. "We can find out then."

"Derek knew where I'd be," Annette said, answering Nancy's question. "But surely *he's* not . . . Derek wouldn't—"

"I'm not accusing him," Nancy said quickly. "I'm just thinking things through."

She glanced at George, who was looking at her with troubled eyes. "I know what you're thinking," George said. "That Kevin knew, too. Maybe he *was* there when we were talking about where to run, but I still don't think . . ." Her voice trailed off, and she stared straight ahead.

Suddenly Annette snapped her fingers. "Nancy, I just remembered! I stopped off at the marathon office on my way to lunch. Someone asked me about good runs in the neighborhood, and I mentioned Grant Park, that I was going there this afternoon. Irene Neff was there at the time—she must have heard me. So was Gina. Either of them could've waited at the fountain until we came by."

"Does notepaper with a marbled design in red ring a bell?" Nancy asked.

Annette shook her head.

"At least we know that there's more than one person involved here," Nancy went on. "There's the shooter, and the person who wrote the note *to* the shooter. So we've learned something."

But we're not learning enough, Nancy added to herself, or fast enough.

At the hotel everyone piled out of the car. "I want you all to stay close until my partner checks that board," said Sergeant Stokes while his partner disappeared through the hotel's entrance. "We're not done here yet."

The three girls waited silently on the sidewalk next to the hotel's curved entrance drive. Detective Zandt returned a moment later.

"The note is gone," he told his partner.

Annette tapped her foot impatiently. "What now?" she asked.

"We'll need to see those anonymous notes," Sergeant Stokes told her. "Then we'll talk to Derek Townsend and, uh, let's see . . ." He consulted a list. "Renee Clark, Irene Neff, Charles Mellor, Gina Giraldi, and Kevin Davis. That'll do, for now."

"I should hope so," Annette muttered. "By the time we're done, the marathon will be over." She glanced up the hotel's drive. "Well, we can at least get started right away. Here comes one of the suspects now."

A light blue car with an ICT placard in the window pulled to a halt behind the police car. Nancy recognized Kevin's face behind the wheel.

She felt a knot twist inside her stomach as she recognized something else—a large scrape on the car's right rear fender.

Kevin was driving the same car the sniper had escaped in!

Chapter
Twelve

As KEVIN GOT OUT of the car, the two officers approached him. "Kevin Davis?" Sergeant Stokes asked.

"That's me," Kevin said cheerfully. Waving at George, Nancy, and Annette, he said, "Hi! How was your run?"

As the officers identified themselves, Kevin looked puzzled. He gave George a questioning look as the group filed into the hotel and headed for a grouping of chairs and a sofa. George smiled encouragingly at him, but Nancy noticed that her eyes were filled with worry.

"I'll find Derek," Annette offered as the others sat down. "He has those anonymous notes."

With a nod Detective Zandt said, "Why don't you wait with him in your room? We'll be up to see you shortly." After giving him her room number, Annette hurried toward the elevators.

"Mind telling us where you've been for the last hour or so?" Sergeant Stokes asked Kevin.

Kevin hesitated before answering. "I was . . . attending to business. Why?"

Why is he being evasive? Nancy wondered.

When the officers told Kevin about the shooting, Kevin looked at George with alarm. "You were there, too! Are you all right?"

George nodded, and Nancy was relieved to note that for once Kevin didn't seem interested in another "little bit of drama" for his big story on Annette. He seemed genuinely concerned for George.

"Mr. Davis, we need to know where you were at the time in question," Detective Zandt went on.

Kevin's mouth fell open. "Am *I* a suspect?"

"Your car matches the one the gunman drove," said Stokes. "The color, the scrape, ICT placard."

"I'd rather not say where I was," Kevin said, suddenly flustered. "But I had nothing to do with any shooting or anything else illegal!"

Detective Zandt hooked his thumbs in the belt loops of his slacks. "How do you explain the car?" he asked Kevin.

"I can't. I only took it fifteen minutes ago. ICT has a pool of cars. You sign a log when you take a car out and when you return it. And you put down the time. Check the log if you want." Kevin pulled a pad and pen from his inside jacket pocket and wrote something down. "Here's the ICT number. Call the office."

"I'll do just that," said Detective Zandt, getting up and heading for the bank of phones near the elevators.

Sergeant Stokes leaned forward in his chair and said to Kevin, "We understand you're covering what's been happening to Annette Lang here. Is it fair to say that the more that happens to her, the better it is for your career?"

"Sure," Kevin replied, shrugging. "We figured that it would be a good thing for both of us."

The sergeant gave Kevin a puzzled look. "And just how would it be good for Annette Lang?"

"Annette wants a shot at a job like mine, in sports broadcasting," Kevin explained. "You see, about a year ago she was given a trial with 'SportsTalk'—that's another cable sports show. But on the first day's taping, she was so nervous that she froze up in front of the camera. The ratings were so bad they never asked her back."

Kevin shook his head ruefully. "It's a pretty cutthroat business. She never got a second chance until now. The ICT brass have been impressed with Annette in the footage we've shot."

Nancy looked at Kevin in surprise. This was news.

"And it looks as if I might be headed to a job with a bigger network show," Kevin went on proudly. "Which means that ICT will be in the market for a track analyst real soon. They'll probably give Annette serious consideration."

Nancy looked up as Detective Zandt returned and sat back down. "I called ICT. Kevin Davis signed the car out at four o'clock, like he says. And he was in the office just before."

"Hmm," said Sergeant Stokes, stroking his long sideburns. "Who had the car before Davis?"

"The log says it was in the garage since eleven this morning. But from what the guy told me, it seems as if security there is pretty lousy. There's just one guy with the cars, and if he leaves, the cars are unattended. The keys just hang there on a numbered board. I got the feeling that it would be easy for someone to take one."

"Let's be reasonable here," Kevin urged. "If I *was* going to commit a crime, would I use a car with an ICT placard?"

Kevin had a point, Nancy had to admit.

The police officers exchanged a look. "All right, Mr. Davis, that's it for now," said Stokes. "But we may want to see you again." He looked at his partner. "Let's find Annette Lang and Derek Townsend."

There was an awkward silence after the officers left. "Uh, excuse me, I have to call my agent," Kevin finally said. He looked at George and squeezed her hand. Then he got up and left the two girls alone.

"George?" Nancy said tentatively. "Nothing would make me happier than if Kevin is innocent. I hope you believe that."

George sat still a moment, then turned toward Nancy. "I know," she said softly. "I guess I couldn't help getting upset about it back in the park. It's just that . . . well, I feel as if there's something really special happening between Kevin and me. And to think that he might have . . ."

Her words trailed off into a huge sigh. "But you're right—a lot of stuff *does* point to him."

"And to Irene Neff and to Gina Giraldi," Nancy reminded George. "We don't know for sure that Kevin *did* do it, either."

George smiled weakly. "Right again, Nan." Her smile brightened as Kevin walked back up to them.

"Great news!" he said. "My agent says that 'Worldwide Sports' wants me to announce for them on a trial basis, starting next month! I'm taking you all out to dinner to celebrate—and I won't take no for an answer!"

George's glum mood seemed to melt away as she looked up into Kevin's handsome face. "It's a date!" she told him. "If that's okay with you, Nan," she added quickly.

"Definitely," Nancy agreed. She could see how important this was to George, and she wasn't about to let down her friend.

"So meet me here at seven-thirty," said Kevin. He hesitated, then asked George, "Would you mind if I talk to Nancy alone a minute?"

"Uh, sure," George agreed. "I'll be over by the message board."

"Listen," Kevin told Nancy once George was out of earshot, "I have no hard feelings about you suspecting me. I know I acted suspiciously just now. I didn't want to say where I was this afternoon because . . . well, I bought George a good-luck gift for the race."

He glanced over his shoulder to be sure George wasn't looking, then retrieved a small box from his jacket pocket and opened it for Nancy. Inside was a thin silver chain from which dangled a small silver charm in the shape of a running shoe.

"Oh, it's darling!" Nancy exclaimed in a low voice. "George is going to love it."

Kevin held a finger up to his lips. "Don't say anything. It's a surprise."

"Your secret is safe with me," Nancy assured him. Kevin looked sincere, and Nancy wanted to believe him—now more than ever. George's happiness depended on it.

"I shouldn't have had the chocolate soufflé," Bess groaned as she, George, Kevin, and Nancy returned to the hotel after dinner. "I'm going to turn into a total blimp."

"If you are, so am I," Nancy told Bess with a laugh, "since I had it, too."

George grinned at her friends. "One thing I love about being in training is carbo-loading. I mean, I ate a huge plate of pasta with pesto sauce, *plus* soup and salad and chocolate cake." Reaching out for Kevin's hand, she said, "Thanks for taking us."

In response, Kevin gave her a kiss on the cheek. "I guess I'd better head home," he said. "Tomorrow's going to be a busy day, what with interviews and prep work for Sunday's race."

"I can't believe it's the day after tomorrow," George said, her eyes glowing with excitement. "I'd better get to bed."

Bess yawned. "After that dinner I'm ready to

call it a night. Thank you, Kevin. It was fabulous."

"My pleasure," he replied. "Good night, all." He kissed George lightly on the lips, then left the hotel.

There was an elevator waiting, and the girls stepped in. When it stopped at the fourth floor, Nancy said, "You two go on. I'll be back in a few minutes."

"What are you doing?" Bess asked, holding open the elevator door after she and George got out.

"I want to see Irene Neff and Gina."

George raised an eyebrow. "Need some help?"

Shaking her head, Nancy replied. "No, thanks. If there are too many of us, they might get defensive."

As the doors slid closed, Nancy considered how to approach the two women. I might as well be direct, she decided. Brenda's already blown my cover. It was ten-thirty, and Gina was probably in bed. If she was caught unprepared, she might let something slip or leave evidence in view.

After getting out on the ninth floor, Nancy made her way to Room 915, which she remembered was Gina's. When she knocked on the door, there was no answer. She knocked again, more loudly. Still nothing.

Gina's breaking training, Nancy thought. On an impulse she got out her lockpicking kit. Seeing that the hallway was deserted, she went to work. A moment later the lock clicked open.

Nancy pushed the door inward, but it would

only go a few inches. The security chain held it closed. Through the narrow opening, Nancy saw that the room was dark.

So she *is* in there, Nancy thought. All I'm finding out is that she's a sound sleeper. As Nancy shut the door, she paused. Was that a noise inside? She froze, listening, but heard nothing else. Probably just my imagination, she decided.

Continuing down the hall, Nancy went to Room 926, Irene Neff's room, and knocked on the door. Irene opened the door and looked surprised to see Nancy.

"What is it? It's late," Irene said coolly.

"We need to talk," Nancy told her. Without giving Irene a chance to say no, Nancy breezed past her and entered the room. There were papers scattered over the table. A coffeepot and a half-full cup sat there as well.

"You know, you're getting to be a pest," Irene snapped. "What do we have to talk about?"

Nancy sat on the couch facing the table. "Did the police see you today?" she asked.

Irene's eyes narrowed. "Yes. I had nothing to tell them—or you."

"These attacks against Annette are getting more intense, and I need to find out a few things," Nancy said, swallowing her irritation.

"From me?" As Neff paced in front of her, Nancy thought she looked more nervous than angry. "Why me? I didn't shoot at her. I've been in meetings all day."

Nancy was about to ask Irene about her day's

schedule when she saw something on the table that made her stop in her tracks.

In the middle of the mess of papers was a distinctive piece of notepaper. It had exactly the same red marbled pattern as the one that had advised the sniper to be at the fountain in Grant Park!

Chapter

Thirteen

Nancy tried not to show her excitement as she took a second glance at the paper.

Wait a minute, Nancy thought. The handwriting on the note was different from the writing she had seen on the marbled paper on the message board, Nancy realized. This was more rounded and vertical.

"I have to finish up some work," Irene said suddenly, looking edgy. "Let's cut this short."

"It won't take long," Nancy assured her.

Irene stopped pacing and faced Nancy. "You don't understand, I'm a busy woman," she snapped. "I don't have time to play detective games with you, so you can just find someone else to pester."

Nancy made no move to get up. "All right," she said. "I suppose you've already told the officers on the case how Annette Lang turned down an endorsement deal with TruForm, which gives you a motive for wanting to hurt her—"

"That's not true!" Irene sputtered.

"I happen to know it *is* true," Nancy countered, without saying how she had found out. Fixing Irene with a steady gaze, she went on. "And I imagine you told the police that your job hinges on Renee Clark winning the Heartland Marathon, so I won't have to mention it to them."

Nancy rose from her chair and said smoothly, "Well, good night, Ms. Neff. Sorry to bother you."

"Wait a minute." Irene's voice was urgent. "What are you saying? Do you really suspect me of being connected with the attacks?"

"You have an interest in eliminating Annette from the race," Nancy said, sitting back down. "And you suggested shopping at the Winning Margin this morning. Someone attacked me there."

Irene sank down on the couch next to Nancy. "But this is absurd! I'm no criminal."

"One other thing," Nancy continued. "There was a note on the message board before Annette, George, and I went out to run. It gave the exact time and place where the shots were fired."

Irene stared blankly at Nancy. "Those detectives said something about that, too. You think *I* wrote the note?"

"It was written on very unusual paper—

97

exactly like that piece," Nancy explained, pointing to the red marbled note. "That isn't your notepaper?"

"Of course not!" Irene reached among the papers on the table and grabbed a sheet of ivory paper with Irene Neff printed at the top. "This is mine."

Nancy kept her eyes fixed on the other woman. "Then whose is this other paper?"

"How should I know? I mean . . . there may be dozens of people who have paper like that." Irene fidgeted nervously with the sheet of personal notepaper she still held.

Shooting Irene a skeptical glance, Nancy said, "You don't know who sent you this note?"

There was a long pause. Finally Irene turned to face Nancy, her mouth set in a grim line. "I won't tell you. I can't."

Nancy stood up. "Ms. Neff, somebody shot at Annette. She might have been killed. This is no time for holding anything back. I thought you might prefer to talk with me in private here, rather than being questioned by the police, but it's up to you, naturally."

Irene leaned into one corner of the couch. She looked trapped. "All right, I'll tell you," she said at last. "But you have to promise not to tell the police."

"I could get in major trouble for withholding evidence of a crime," Nancy told her. "But I'll promise not to tell the police if it isn't necessary. That's the best I can do."

Ms. Neff sighed deeply, then said, "The note

was from Renee, but I can't believe she'd do anything criminal. She can hardly bring herself to make a rival runner feel bad by beating her in a race."

This tallied with what Jake Haitinck had told her and Bess about Renee Clark the night before at the dance club. "Is this her regular style of notepaper?" Nancy asked.

"I've gotten one or two other memos from her on it, but I don't know if she has a lot of it or not. I don't know . . . really!"

Nancy took another look at the note. "This is definitely not the handwriting that was on the message board," she said, thinking aloud. "Can you think of someone else who might have persuaded Renee to improve her chances by starting this campaign against Annette? Gina, possibly? Charles Mellor?"

"I cannot imagine Renee having something to do with anything illegal under any circumstances. Period."

Nancy's gut instinct told her that Irene was telling her the truth. She thought for a moment, then asked, "What about Charles Mellor? How did he become Renee's trainer?"

"Her old trainer retired two years ago," Irene explained. "Renee was just another runner then, nothing special. Charles came up after a race and started giving her tips, and she listened. Next thing, he was her trainer, and she was a major contender."

Nancy stood up. "Okay. That's all for now."

Irene clasped her hands nervously together as

she, too, rose from the couch. "You're not going to bother Renee with this now, are you? She needs her sleep."

Nancy paused. "What about Charles Mellor?"

"You can give him a try," Irene said, gesturing to her phone.

Nancy got no answer from Mellor's room. It was now after eleven, so she decided to call it a night.

When she got back to her room, Bess and George were already asleep in their beds. After changing into her nightshirt, Nancy slipped between the sheets of the cot, but she had a hard time falling asleep.

The race was the day after tomorrow, and she didn't feel any closer to finding who was after Annette. If she didn't make some progress—and quickly—the Heartland Marathon might be the last race Annette Lang ever ran.

"Good morning, sleepyhead."

Nancy heard Bess's cheerful voice and rolled over onto her stomach. "Hrmphh," she mumbled sleepily.

"Come on. George is already working out at the gym, and I'm starving. Get up, Drew."

Cracking open one eye, Nancy saw that Bess was perched on the edge of her bed, her arms crossed over the oversize pink cotton sweater she was wearing with white leggings.

"Okay, okay," Nancy said, pushing the covers aside and swinging her feet to the floor. "Just give me a few minutes to get dressed.

Fifteen minutes later Nancy had showered and

was dressed in jeans and a blue pullover. "Ready," she said, grabbing her shoulder bag.

As they got into the elevator, Bess said, "After that dinner last night, I'm definitely on a diet today. I'll have poached eggs, not fried, without bacon. And less toast, with no—well, only a little—butter."

Nancy was chuckling as the elevator doors opened into the lobby. Her smile disappeared, however, when she saw Brenda Carlton standing there, looking annoyed.

"Have you seen Gina Giraldi?" Brenda asked as Nancy and Bess got off the elevator.

"Good morning to you, too, Brenda," said Nancy. "And no, I haven't. Why?"

Brenda frowned. "We were supposed to meet for that interview a half hour ago. Nobody's seen her, and when I tried calling her room, there was no answer."

"Maybe she went somewhere and got delayed," Bess suggested. "Or maybe she forgot about it."

"*Forgot* about it?" Brenda repeated, glaring at Bess. "Forgot about an interview with a *major* paper? I don't think so."

Nancy rolled her eyes. *Today's Times* was hardly a "major paper." Trust Brenda to exaggerate her own importance.

Still, Brenda's words triggered a slight tingle of concern in Nancy. Gina didn't seem like the kind of person who would miss out on a chance to get newspaper coverage.

"Let's go knock on her door," Nancy suggested.

Nancy, Bess, and Brenda took the elevator to the ninth floor and went to Gina's room. Nancy knocked on the door. There was no answer.

"Now what?" asked Bess.

In response Nancy took out her lockpicking kit and began to probe the lock.

"Hmm. I see you've learned a trade from all those criminals you go after," Brenda remarked snidely.

Nancy didn't bother to answer. A moment later there was a click, and Gina's door opened. The shades were drawn, and the room was in shadow.

"Hello?" Nancy called. "Gina?"

There was no answer. Stepping forward, Nancy flipped on the lights. Bess and Brenda were right behind her.

Nancy froze at the sight before her. Behind her, Brenda and Bess both let out horrified cries.

Gina lay stretched out on the floor, unconscious, an ugly, dark bruise on her forehead.

Chapter

Fourteen

Nancy fought back the wave of nausea that swept over her. She hurried over to Gina and quickly checked her pulse. It was there but very weak.

"She's alive. Call the house doctor and an ambulance," she said to Bess and Brenda, who stood stiffly by the door.

Bess nodded and went to the phone. Brenda sat on the bed, looking as if she might faint.

"Don't touch anything in here," Nancy cautioned. Suddenly a chilling thought hit her.

When she had tried to get into Gina's room the night before, the security chain had been on. It could only have been fastened from *inside* the room. For all she knew, the attacker could have been going after Gina at the exact moment that Nancy had been there!

Nancy pushed away the awful thought as Bess hung up the phone and announced, "The doctor and paramedics are on the way." Looking at Gina, she added, "I guess I'd better call the police, too."

She picked up the phone again and dialed. After a brief conversation, Bess hung up and turned to Nancy. "Sergeant Stokes says they'll be here in ten minutes and not to touch anything."

Before long, Gina's room was filled with paramedics, the hotel's doctor, and a crowd of police technicians accompanied by Sergeant Stokes and Detective Zandt.

"Looks like a serious concussion," said the hotel doctor. "We won't know how serious, however, until I run some tests and take X-rays at the hospital."

Nancy, Bess, and Brenda looked on as the paramedics carefully laid Gina on a gurney and wheeled her out. Curious onlookers were urged to move away by a guard at the door.

While Detective Zandt directed the police technicians in dusting for fingerprints and looking for clues, Sergeant Stokes led Nancy, Bess, and Brenda over to a quiet spot near the door. They told him all they remembered about finding Gina.

"Annette Lang has been the main target until this," Sergeant Stokes said. "Any idea why someone would go after Gina Giraldi?"

"Gina planned to give a story to Brenda," Nancy explained, nodding at the reporter. "She was going to expose some crooked dealings by someone connected with the Heartland Marathon."

Stokes scribbled notes and nodded.

"Brenda bragged to me about her scoop yesterday," Nancy went on, "in front of a number of people—Renee Clark, Charles Mellor, Irene Neff, Kevin Davis . . . I don't remember who else. She said specifically that Gina was going to name names."

"Is that so?" Stokes said, giving Brenda a sharp look. "Not too smart, ma'am."

Brenda glared at Nancy but said nothing.

The police sergeant tapped his pad with his pen. "Someone is at large who was desperate enough to try to shut Gina Giraldi's mouth permanently to keep something secret," he said. "He or she might try the same thing on you and your friends. So watch out. You could be in danger."

He looked at Brenda again. "That goes double for you."

"What do you mean?" Brenda asked indignantly.

Nancy answered for the sergeant. "The person who attacked Gina can't be sure that she didn't *already* talk to you. So you might know things you shouldn't. If I were you, I'd watch my back."

"And learn to keep your mouth shut," Sergeant Stokes added. "Otherwise, you can get people into trouble, including yourself."

Brenda nodded, but there was a defiant look in her eyes. She still didn't seem to recognize the seriousness of her slip.

"Now," said Stokes, consulting his notes. "We got preliminary statements yesterday from Irene Neff, Renee Clark, Annette Lang, Charles Mellor, and Kevin Davis. I'm going to need to know their whereabouts for last night, too."

It took some doing, but Sergeant Stokes managed to find everyone. Renee Clark and Charles Mellor were at the gym, but Irene and Kevin both had to be tracked down at their offices. Annette was on a run, so the police officer left a message for her at the front desk, asking her to join them when she returned.

An hour later everyone but Annette and Kevin was assembled in the lobby. George had joined them, too, when she returned to the hotel after her workout.

Sergeant Stokes decided not to delay questioning any longer. Taking Nancy, Bess, and George aside, he said, "I'd like you to be here, too. See if what they say fits with what you know."

As the sergeant led them into the empty press room, Brenda Carlton started in as well.

"Where are you going?" Stokes asked, barring her way.

"I thought I'd sit in," Brenda said with a smile that faded quickly under Stokes's glare.

"You thought wrong. This isn't an open forum for your gossip column. It's police business."

Red-faced, Brenda turned and left the room.

Stokes stood in front of the three suspects, who sat on the room's couch. Nancy, Bess, and George stood off to the side.

"Sometime late last night, Gina Giraldi was attacked by someone. She sustained serious head injuries and is unconscious in the hospital at this very moment."

Nancy studied the suspects' reactions as they heard this news. They all looked shocked.

"You can't think any of us had something to do with this?" Renee asked.

"We'll be talking to a number of people," said the sergeant, avoiding a direct answer. "There may be a link between what happened to Gina and some ugly attacks on Annette Lang lately."

"That car that almost ran Annette over," Renee said softly. "I saw that—it was awful!"

"That and other things," said the sergeant. He paused as Annette entered the room, still dressed in her sliver-and-black running outfit.

Nancy noticed that the runner appeared shaken. Her eyes darted every which way, and her hands were clasped together so tightly that her knuckles were white.

"Please join us, Ms. Lang," Sergeant Stokes said.

"Is it true, what I heard about Gina?" Annette asked in a shaky voice, sitting down on an upholstered chair.

The police officer nodded. "It's true."

"So what do you want with me?" Annette asked.

"Give me a break!" Irene burst out. " 'What do you want with me?' " she mimicked. "As if everyone didn't know you hate Gina. You're what's called a *suspect,* Annette."

"I'm a suspect?" Anger replaced the worry in Annette's face. "If there's a logical suspect around here, you're it. If Gina was planning to

expose any dirty linen, yours would be at the top of the bag."

"What is that supposed to mean?" Irene demanded, standing up.

Nancy saw Sergeant Stokes listening quietly. Questioning suspects this way might be unorthodox, but Nancy now realized that the sergeant had probably done it intentionally. Things might be blurted out in anger that wouldn't be said otherwise.

"It means that you're the most likely one to have organized a conspiracy against me," Annette shot back. She turned to Stokes and explained. "She's had it in for me ever since I turned down an endorsement contract for TruForm, and she'll do anything to improve Renee's chances of winning."

"That's a lie!" Irene took a step forward, but Sergeant Stokes stopped her with a gesture.

At that moment Kevin walked into the room. He seemed taken aback by the tension and hostility and said nothing as he took a seat across from Annette.

Irene picked up where she had left off. "It's true, I did talk to Annette about endorsing TruForm, but I'm *glad* she turned us down. Renee is the runner we want. We don't need to sabotage you, Annette. Renee will beat you fair and square!"

"Why are you making these accusations against Irene?" Renee suddenly jumped into the argument and faced Annette. "You have no proof —you're just doing it to hurt her. I used to admire you, Annette, but now I think you're just selfish and malicious. I'm going to *enjoy* beating you tomorrow."

Annette smiled. "Talk is cheap, Renee. You're going to eat those words."

"All right, that'll do," the sergeant interrupted, raising both hands to stop the flow of accusations. "This is all very interesting, but I have some questions to ask everyone before you can go. I want you all to tell me where you were between nine last night and eight this morning. Let's start with you, Ms. Neff."

"I was in my room, working until one-thirty. Then I went to sleep. I came down for breakfast with Renee and Charles at seven-thirty."

Renee had gone to sleep early. She was up at six-thirty, did some light exercise in her room, and met Irene and her trainer in the lobby at seven-thirty. Kevin had gone home after having dinner with George and her friends, and Mellor and Annette stated that they had been in their rooms the whole night. No one had any witnesses.

Sergeant Stokes sighed. "This certainly hasn't gotten us anywhere. I'm giving you all my phone number. If any of you wants to tell me something in confidence, just call. For the moment that'll be all. Ms. Drew, stick around a second."

"We'll wait outside," Bess whispered as she and George filed out with the others. When the press room was empty, Sergeant Stokes turned to Nancy.

"I called the River Heights police and spoke to the chief there—McGinnis, I think it was," Stokes said. "He tells me you're not just a meddling busybody, that I can trust you. So I will. Do you have *anything* to add about what's going on here?"

"Nothing," Nancy answered. "Are you doing background checks on the suspects?"

The sergeant nodded. "They're in progress. I should have results today. I'll keep you informed, and I assume you'll do the same."

"You can count on it," Nancy assured him.

As soon as she rejoined her friends outside the press room, Bess grabbed her arm. "There's something we have to do right away," she said.

"What?" Nancy asked.

"We need to have breakfast—before I starve to death!"

"How was your run, George?" Bess asked that afternoon when George returned.

"Short but great," George replied. Nancy and Bess were sitting on the terrace, and George had gone out to join them. "I just wanted to run enough to keep limber, and I met up with a group of runners like me who're doing their first marathon. We're getting together later for a big carbo-loading dinner. Any news on Gina?"

Nancy shook her head. She had called the Good Samaritan Hospital, where Gina had been taken, a few times. All they could tell her was that Gina was still unconscious.

The phone rang just then, and Nancy went into the room to get it. "Are you busy?" Annette asked. "There's something I need to talk to you about."

"Sure," Nancy said. "Is something wrong?"

There was a slight pause. "Could you come downstairs and meet me in the lobby?"

Nancy agreed, but she was frowning as she hung up the phone. "Annette wants to talk to me downstairs," she told Bess and George. "She wouldn't say what it's about, but I have a feeling it's not good news."

"Maybe Bess and I should come, in case there's some kind of trouble," George suggested.

"Definitely," Bess agreed.

In the lobby Annette greeted them with a nervous smile. "Let's go outside, where we won't be overheard."

Nancy looked around. The lobby wasn't very crowded, and nobody was paying them any particular attention. But Annette appeared to be on edge, so Nancy decided to humor her. The runner was under a lot of strain, after all.

"Is something wrong?" Nancy asked as Annette led her, Bess, and George out of the Woodville and down the hotel's curved drive.

Annette nodded and said, "It's about what's been happening the last few days."

"What?" Nancy asked. Her concern grew as she noticed Annette's pale face and red-rimmed eyes.

Suddenly a squeal of tires made Nancy spin around.

A beat-up car had swung its nose toward the sidewalk just behind them. Nancy realized with a start that it was the same car that had tried to run down Annette in the park!

The passenger door flew open, and a man clothed entirely in black jumped out. His face was covered by a ski mask.

Before Nancy, her friends, or passersby on the busy street could react, the man sprinted up behind Annette and grabbed her around the throat with his left arm. With his right he twisted her arm sharply behind her back and dragged her toward the waiting car!

Chapter

Fifteen

ANNETTE LET OUT a scream of terror that spurred Nancy into action.

She leapt forward as the struggling pair neared the car and kicked sharply at the side of the attacker's knee. There was a muffled cry of pain from behind the ski mask, and the man dropped Annette's arm to clutch his leg.

Nancy lunged for the mask, but the assailant jumped back out of her reach. As he did so, Annette was pulled off-balance, and she fell to the ground, out of the assailant's grasp.

The masked person dived headfirst into the front seat and slammed the car door shut. Several passersby were spurred into action and headed toward the car. Before they or Nancy could get to it, the car took off down the drive and swung out into the busy downtown traffic. Even through the tinted glass, Nancy could see that the assailant was at the wheel. Then the car was gone, leaving an angry blare of horns behind it.

"That's the same car that the person who shot at us was driving," Nancy said.

"And that was definitely a man," George said.

"Yes, it was," Nancy said.

A few feet away several people were helping Annette to her feet. "How are you?" Nancy asked, going over to the runner. "Are you all right?"

"Fine, thanks to you," Annette replied. "I owe you again, Nancy."

"No problem," Nancy told her with a smile. "All part of the service."

The crowd that had formed dispersed. Suddenly Nancy noticed that Brenda Carlton was standing outside the hotel's entrance. An expensive-looking camera was hanging from the reporter's neck, and she was talking into a portable tape recorder in her hand.

"Boy, Brenda doesn't lose any time getting a story—" Nancy muttered. Then she broke off as another thought occurred to her.

"Don't go anywhere," she told Annette. "I'll be right back."

Nancy hurried over to Brenda and asked, "Did you see what just happened?"

"Naturally," Brenda said, giving Nancy a satisfied smile. "And I got great pictures, too. My editor is going to love this."

Something about the reporter's timely appearance seemed very fishy to Nancy. "Why were you out here, Brenda?" she asked.

Brenda attempted a casual shrug, but it didn't look convincing. "I just happened to be outside."

"Just happened?" Nancy repeated, crossing her arms over her chest. "Come on, Brenda, try again."

"I don't know what you're talking about," Brenda said indignantly.

"You never carry a camera—you're not a photographer. Come on, Brenda, let's have it."

Glaring at Nancy, Brenda said, "Well, so what if someone called me? I don't see what difference that makes."

Nancy resisted the urge to shake the reporter. "Tell me all about it."

"There's not much to tell," Brenda said airily. "I was in my room, and the phone rang and someone said that if I wanted a good item, I should be in front of the hotel with a camera in five minutes."

So someone *had* warned Brenda. But who? The attacker seemed like the logical person—no one else would know what was going to happen. But why would the person *want* to get publicity and risk being identified? It didn't make sense.

"The caller didn't give a name?" Nancy asked.

"Of course not," Brenda answered. "Reporters get anonymous tips like that all the time."

Ignoring Brenda's snooty attitude, Nancy asked, "You couldn't tell if it was a man or a woman?"

Brenda held up her hands. "Funny, now that I think about it, I can't say. The voice sounded whispery."

Stifling her disappointment, Nancy thanked Brenda and walked back to Annette, George, and Bess. They were still waiting on the sidewalk where the attacker had let go of Annette.

"Where's Kevin?" Annette was asking George. "I want to tell him what just happened and get it on tape fast, while it's still fresh in my mind."

At the runner's words Nancy stopped dead in her tracks. Annette didn't seem at all shaken up anymore. She actually seemed excited.

Thinking back, Nancy remembered the calm way Annette had handled just about all the threats and attacks. Suddenly things were starting to make sense.

"Kevin can wait a minute," Nancy told Annette. "Now, what was it you wanted to tell me?"

Annette stared blankly at Nancy. "Tell you?"

"That's right," Nancy said patiently. "You called me because you had something to tell me. Then you insisted we go out front where we wouldn't be overheard. Remember?"

"Oh, right—of course." Annette seemed flustered. "I guess nearly getting snatched like that scrambled my brains a little. I'm not thinking straight."

"Take your time," Nancy urged. "You said that you wanted to tell me something about what's been happening to you for the last few days."

Annette's eyes were on Nancy, but they weren't

focused. "Yes, I did. I think Renee and Irene are working together to force me out of the race."

This was nothing new—certainly nothing to drag Nancy outside for. "I see. Is there something that makes them the most likely candidates?"

"Well, yes." Annette swung around to include Bess and George in the conversation. "When those policemen were questioning us this morning, did you notice how Renee jumped up and said that she was going to *enjoy* beating me tomorrow?"

"Yes, I heard her," Nancy replied. "What about it?"

"Don't you see?" Annette fixed Nancy and her friends with an almost pleading look. "She *has* to be part of the conspiracy. She dropped that Goody Two-shoes front she likes to put on and let the *real* Renee show through."

"And that's what you couldn't say inside because someone might overhear it?" Nancy asked.

"Yes," Annette replied. She smiled triumphantly, as if she had just solved the whole case.

Actually, Annette *had* provided Nancy with an important clue, but it had nothing to do with Renee Clark. "I'll keep that in mind," Nancy told the runner. "Let's go back inside."

"What are you getting at?" George whispered to Nancy as they entered the hotel.

"Not now," Nancy whispered back. "You'll find out in a minute."

When the girls were halfway across the lobby, Derek Townsend emerged from the elevator. He hurried over to Annette, his face gray with tension. "Annette," he said, grasping both her hands. "That reporter, Brenda something, just told me what happened. This is terrible!"

"I'm fine, Derek, really I am." Annette disengaged her hands from his and smiled at him.

"Maybe you *should* withdraw from this race," the trainer said. "It's not worth your life to compete, is it?"

"That's out of the question, Derek," Annette insisted, her eyes flashing. "No conspiracy is going to force me out, and that's final. Now I'm going up to change, and then we'll go to the gym for a light workout."

Derek Townsend opened his mouth to object, but Annette had already walked away and was stepping into an open elevator.

"I don't know what to do anymore," he said, turning to Nancy, Bess, and George.

His haggard expression made Nancy realize the toll these last few days had taken on him. She felt sorry for him. She had a feeling the questions she needed to ask weren't going to help his mood any, either.

"Let's sit down and talk for a minute," Nancy suggested. She led Annette's trainer to a nook with two couches facing each other. Nancy sat next to him on one, while George and Bess settled in opposite.

"Mr. Townsend," Nancy began, "give me your honest assessment of Annette's condition. How does she stand up against the best of her rivals? This is just between us, you understand."

The trainer seemed puzzled and hesitated

slightly before answering. "I would say she is certainly still among the best there is, but a number of excellent runners have come up lately. As a result, Annette is no longer in a class by herself, which she was until recently. Renee Clark and a few others are on a par with her."

"So there's no certainty that Annette would win tomorrow, even without these distractions?" George spoke up.

Mr. Townsend shook his head. "No, not at all. It might end up being simply a question of who wants it the most."

Nancy drummed her fingers against the couch arm. "Annette must be thinking about what's next—after she stops running, I mean," she said, "we've heard she'd like to get into sports broadcasting."

Derek chuckled and shook his head. "She did want to, but I'm afraid a fiasco with 'SportsTalk' ruined her chances there."

Obviously, Annette's trainer wasn't aware that the runner might have a second chance at sportscasting.

"I suppose Annette would do about anything for a job like Kevin Davis's," Nancy went on.

"I'll say. Why—" He broke off and gave Nancy a bewildered look. "What's the point of all this?"

Leaning forward, Nancy said, "Mr. Townsend, I'm going to put your mind at ease about the danger to Annette. But I must insist that you keep what I tell you completely to yourself for now."

"Very well," he agreed.

"I'm almost certain that Annette can run tomorrow without fear of being attacked."

"Why?" he demanded. Bess and George were equally mystified.

"Because the conspiracy against Annette was organized by Annette herself!"

Chapter

Sixteen

THE TRAINER gaped at Nancy. "No!" he exclaimed. "It's simply not possible."

"That's totally bizarre," Bess whispered.

"But it *is* possible," Nancy insisted. "In fact, it should have been clear to me all along. No one has a stronger motive for harassing Annette Lang than Annette herself.

"Mr. Townsend, Annette is already finding it crowded at the top. These so-called attacks have been getting her a big dose of media exposure. Kevin says that she pressed him to put in a good word for her with the ICT execs. This is just the break she needs, only she maneuvered it herself."

The man frowned but said nothing.

"I had suspected Kevin Davis of using Annette

for career advancement, but it's actually the other way around." Nancy caught George's triumphant look and smiled back.

"Annette could have prepared the anonymous notes, ripped up her own gear, even attacked me in the changing booth," Nancy went on. "I thought it was odd when she asked me to join her on her trip to the store, since she'd been resisting my attempts to protect her. Now I know why she wanted me along."

"But what about Gina Giraldi?" Derek protested. "Surely Annette wouldn't let someone be seriously hurt, or even killed, for the sake of a career. She's not as cold-blooded as that!"

Nancy had been wondering about that herself. "Well, we know she's not doing all this by herself," she said, thinking out loud. "The note on the message board means she's got an accomplice. I guess it's possible that that person has gotten out of control."

"That's right," Bess put in. "Annette really *did* seem upset after finding out about Gina. That was about the only time she ever lost her cool."

Nancy nodded. "Except for when I went after that sniper," she remembered. "I thought she was worried about *me,* but what she was really worried about was that I might catch her accomplice."

"Gee," George said, shaking her head. "Who do you think the accomplice is?"

"I wish I knew, because whoever it is is a very dangerous person," Nancy replied. "I don't think it's Renee or Irene anymore. One, Annette is trying too hard to implicate them. Two, the person who 'attacked' Annette today was definitely a man."

Turning to Mr. Townsend, Nancy asked, "By the way, do you have a sample of Annette's handwriting?"

"I have a note here, actually," he replied, pulling a piece of paper from his pocket and passing it to Nancy. It was a note setting the time of that afternoon's gym workout.

Nancy looked at it and frowned. The script didn't resemble the backhanded writing of the note she had seen on the message board.

"Hey, Nan," Bess spoke up. "How did you figure out about Annette?"

"She didn't set up this so-called abduction attempt very well. She drags us outside as witnesses and calls Brenda's room to ensure press coverage. But when I ask her what she wants to tell me, she has nothing new to say."

"Astonishing," the trainer said quietly. "I'd never have thought it, but listening to you, it all fits."

"Now what?" Bess wanted to know. "Do we go to Annette and make her say who she's working with?"

"I don't think so," Nancy said. "The accomplice is already dangerous. Knowing we're on the trail might make things even more dangerous. I'd like to check a few more things first, before confronting Annette."

"Such as?" George asked.

"Let's call the hospital and check on Gina again," Nancy answered. "If she can talk, she might identify her attacker. Mr. Townsend, I know this is hard for you since you're Annette's trainer. But can you behave toward Annette as if you don't know anything of what we've been talking about?"

The man nodded. "I'll do my best."

Leaving the trainer, Nancy, George, and Bess headed across the lobby toward the phones near the elevators.

"Ms. Drew?" A clerk at the desk motioned to Nancy as the girls passed by. "A call came in for you a few minutes ago. Here's the message."

He handed her a slip of paper that said, "Call Sergeant Stokes." A number was listed beneath.

Nancy hurried over to the bank of phones, and her friends followed. She dialed the number but was told that Stokes was out. She then called the hospital. A nurse informed her that Gina was drifting in and out of consciousness and had said a few words.

Nancy relayed the news to Bess and George. "I think it's worth a shot at trying to talk to Gina."

"I'm willing," said Bess. "Let's go."

George held back. "Would you guys mind if I don't go?" she asked. "There's that early carbo-loading dinner in the restaurant tonight, and then Kevin said he has something special to give me." George's voice lowered as she said the last part, and she gave Nancy and Bess an embarrassed smile.

"No problem," Nancy told George. "Have fun!"

George offered to let them use her car, which was parked in the hotel garage, but Nancy and Bess decided to take a cab to the hospital. They got Gina's room number from the reception desk. On the third floor a nurse directed them to Gina's room.

"She might not make much sense," the nurse warned them. "It's mostly just babble."

The two girls paused just inside the door of the room. Gina's head was wrapped in bandages, and underneath her eyes were huge, ugly bruises.

Bess shook her head angrily. "Whoever did this deserves to—" She broke off as the runner's eyes fluttered open and her lips moved.

Nancy and Bess hurried over to Gina's bedside and bent over to listen.

"Monk . . ." came a faint whisper. "I know him. . . . It was monk . . ." Then she closed her eyes.

"Monk?" repeated Bess, looking at Nancy. "That nurse was right—she *is* just babbling."

"Maybe," Nancy admitted. "Anyway, it looks as if Gina is out again for now. We might as well go back to the hotel. I'll try Sergeant Stokes again. Maybe 'monk' will mean something to him."

"Not there?" Bess guessed an hour and a half later, when Nancy hung up the phone in their room.

Nancy nodded. It was the third time since returning from the hospital that she had tried to contact Sergeant Stokes. Each time she had been told he was out and couldn't be reached. "My stomach's growling," she said. "Let's go eat dinner."

Just then the door opened, and George walked

in. "Look at this!" she exclaimed, holding up the silver running shoe charm Kevin had shown Nancy the day before.

"How cute!" Bess exclaimed, examining it.

"Kevin gave it to me as a good-luck charm for the race tomorrow. *That's* why he didn't want to say where he was yesterday. He wanted to surprise me. Isn't he wonderful?"

Nancy smiled at George. "He really is," she agreed. "Hey, it's only seven-thirty. How come you're not still out with Mr. Wonderful?"

"I have to be up by six-thirty tomorrow morning," George told her. "The race starts at nine, and I should be there by seven-thirty or eight. So tonight I'm not doing anything but sleeping."

After saying good night to George, Nancy and Bess left the room and went to the Great Fire for dinner.

"I never thought I'd feel sorry for Gina," Bess said, taking a bite of her chicken crepes, "but now I do. What a terrible thing to happen."

Nancy frowned and speared a lettuce leaf with her fork. "I just hope we can make sure the same thing doesn't happen to anybody else," she said. Looking up, she noticed a familiar, curly blond head a few tables away.

"Oh, there's Jake," she said. "He doesn't seem too happy." The runner's association official was staring down at his dessert and coffee without touching them.

"Poor Jake. He's probably upset about Gina," Bess said sympathetically. "I'm going to ask him to join us."

She got up and went over to his table. A

moment later Bess returned with Jake, who was carrying his cup of espresso and his dessert plate.

"I am happy for company," he told them. "It saves me from thinking about Gina's terrible ordeal."

Nancy and Bess told him about their visit, trying to make Gina's condition sound as hopeful as possible. They didn't say anything about her mention of "monk."

Jake seemed grateful when Bess launched into a humorous story about George's many failed attempts to get her to take up running. By the end of the meal he was even laughing. When they left the restaurant and said good night, Nancy felt good about the friendship that had begun between them.

She and Bess were headed for the phones to call Sergeant Stokes again when Nancy heard Renee Clark calling her name.

"Nancy! Over here!" Renee was standing by the message board.

Nancy raised her eyebrows at Bess, and the two girls crossed the lobby to the runner.

"All set for tomorrow?" Nancy asked Renee.

"More or less," Renee said distractedly. Nancy noticed that her usual cheery attitude was gone. Actually, Renee appeared very worried.

"Have you seen Charles around anywhere? My trainer?" the runner asked.

Nancy shook her head. "Not since this morning," she answered.

Renee frowned. "We were supposed to have dinner together tonight and go over my strategy for tomorrow. But he's not anywhere around. I called his room several times, but there's no answer, and nobody has seen him since early in the day."

"Maybe he was delayed somewhere," Bess suggested.

"Well, there *was* a note from him on the board," Renee went on, "and in it he said he might be late. But it's so strange that he wouldn't have dinner with me tonight, when I have such an important race tomorrow." She pulled a folded piece of paper from her pocket.

Nancy stared at the note, stunned. It was the red-marbled notepaper!

"Can I see that for a second?" she asked.

"Sure," said Renee, handing it over.

Her pulse racing, Nancy read the brief message: "I may be a little late tonight. If I am, don't wait for me. C."

There was no mistaking that distinctive back-slanted scrawl. It was definitely the same as the handwriting in the note giving the details of the sniper shooting.

And that meant that Charles Mellor was Annette's accomplice—and that *he* had staged where the shooting should take place!

Chapter

Seventeen

Renee, is this Mellor's regular notepaper?"
Nancy asked.

Renee nodded. "It's from somewhere in Europe. Charles lived there for years, and he still
has this stuff imported."

"And this is his handwriting?" Nancy pressed.

"Definitely," Renee replied without hesitation. "It's pretty distinctive, isn't it, that backward tilt? He writes left-handed, so—"

"Excuse me," Nancy said, cutting off Renee. "Bess and I have an important phone call to make."

As soon as they left Renee, Nancy told Bess what she had just discovered. "You're sure it's him?" Bess asked, her eyes wide.

Nancy nodded firmly. She reached for the nearest receiver when they got to the bank of telephones in the lobby. This time she got through to Sergeant Stokes.

"I have important news," said the sergeant.

"I do, too, and I suspect it fits in with yours," Nancy said over the line. "Let's hear yours first."

"Okay. The only one on your list of suspects who didn't check out squeaky clean was Charles Mellor. His fingerprints rang bells in our computers. According to Interpol, he has a criminal record under another name, Calvin Munk—M-u-n-k."

"'Monk!' Of course!" Nancy exclaimed. "Let me guess," she went on excitedly. "I'll bet Calvin Munk's criminal record has to do with professional track or distance running in Europe."

"Right you are," Stokes answered, sounding surprised. "He was banned from racing in Europe for doctoring some runner's food before a race. He knew his chemistry—he added some poisonous mushrooms to the chicken in wine sauce the guy had ordered. Made the guy sick as a dog. It was supposed to look like food poisoning."

"There's something else, too," Nancy said. She told the detective about Gina saying "Munk" at the hospital. "And Renee Clark just identified the handwriting on the note that had the time and place of the shooting in the park. Charles Munk wrote it."

Stokes made a low whistle.

"Gina and Annette have both been around for a while, and they both have run on the European circuit," Nancy went on. "Gina must have recognized Mellor as Munk from back then."

"That makes sense," the sergeant agreed. "If he thought she was going to talk to Brenda Carlton about some scandal involving him, he might have figured he had to stop her."

"That's another thing," Nancy said. "Munk is half of the conspiracy responsible for all the incidents we've been investigating."

There was a pause before Stokes said, "And I suppose you've worked out who the other half is?"

"It's Annette herself," Nancy told him. She went on to explain her theory that the whole thing was to build up Annette's TV exposure so that she would be hired as a sportscaster.

"And that's who Monk left the note for. He was telling her where to run so that he could set up the shooting. Originally I thought that the note was *for* the sniper, but it was *from* Munk to Annette."

"It *does* fit," Sergeant Stokes said slowly. "Between them they had the means, the motive, and the opportunity for everything. Munk must have been driving the car that was used in the apparent hit-and-run and the so-called abduction attempt."

"And he 'borrowed' ICT cars in all three instances, probably to throw suspicion on Kevin in case he was seen."

"The question is, what was his motive?" Stokes wondered aloud. "What did Munk gain?"

Nancy paused for a moment, thinking. "My hunch is that Annette blackmailed him into helping her. Like Gina, she must have recognized him. She would have known what he had done in Europe and she probably threatened to expose him. The problem is, he's vanished."

After a short silence, Sergeant Stokes said, "Stay put. My partner and I are on the way."

Nancy felt a sinking feeling in the pit of her stomach when the hotel's concierge let her, Bess, Sergeant Stokes, and Detective Zandt into Calvin Munk's room ten minutes later.

"He's already gotten away, hasn't he," Bess said, leaning against the wall next to the door. Empty drawers stuck out of the dresser, and the closet held nothing but some hangers.

"Looks that way," said Sergeant Stokes.

"Take a look at this," Detective Zandt called to his partner as he peered inside the top dresser drawer. He held up two brass rifle cartridges.

Sergeant Stokes examined them. "The same kind the sniper used in the park," he said. Then he went back to searching the area near the bed.

"Well, well." Sergeant Stokes pulled a pad of the marbled notepaper from the bedside table. He held it close to the bedside lamp. "Indentations on the top sheet," he observed. "Munk wrote something down and tore off the sheet."

Nancy went over and watched while he did a pencil rubbing. "A phone number," she said.

The sergeant nodded. "We'll get out an all-points bulletin on Munk," he said, "and we'll check on this number."

"He could still be planning more attacks,"

Detective Zandt said. "If Munk wants to bury his past, he'll go after Annette. That reporter—"

"Brenda Carlton," Nancy supplied.

"Right. She's another possible target. We can keep watch on her, but I don't see how we can keep an eye on Annette along the whole marathon route. We should just put her into custody right now and be done with it."

Nancy held up a hand. "The problem is that Annette's arrest will make news. When Munk hears of it, he'll go into hiding."

"But if she isn't arrested, Munk is bound to be somewhere on that marathon course tomorrow, waiting for her," Bess put in, picking up on Nancy's reasoning.

"Right," the sergeant said. "And we can't possibly cover over twenty-six miles. It would take an army."

"Munk has dropped out of sight and changed identities once before," Nancy pointed out. "If he runs for it, he may be able to do it again."

Sergeant Stokes sighed and scratched his head. "We might be able to arrange to have a police scooter trail Annette along the course. I'll check with the racing association. I'll make my final decision in the morning."

"For now we'll put a discreet guard on Annette's and Brenda's rooms," Detective Zandt added.

Checking her watch, Nancy saw that it was after ten. "Let's tell George what's been happening," she said to Bess.

They said good night to Stokes and Zandt, then

went down a flight to their room. When they opened the door, the room was dark, but Nancy saw George stir in her bed.

"I was just drifting off," George said groggily, sitting up and turning on the bedside light. "Are you guys going to sleep already?"

Bess went over and sat on the edge of her cousin's bed. "We know who Annette's accomplice is," she told George in a rush. "Charles Mellor, except his name is really Calvin Munk."

"Slow down," George urged, holding up both palms. "Charles Mellor is the other half of Annette's conspiracy? You mean, Renee Clark's trainer? What did you say his real name is?"

Nancy quickly told George about the history of Calvin Munk and that he had written the note on the message board. "Now Munk has disappeared, and the police are afraid he might try to hide the truth about his past by killing Annette tomorrow."

"In the race?" George sat bolt upright, now fully awake. "But how? Where? There'll be thousands of people watching, and television crews and everything. Annette is going to be in front of a TV camera for most of the race. He'd be crazy to try anything."

"Maybe he *is* crazy," Bess suggested.

Nancy nodded thoughtfully. "One thing's for sure. He's getting more and more out of control. What he did to Gina shows that he's no longer going to worry about hurting people."

George's eyes widened. "How can we help?"

"Right now the police are taking care of everything," Nancy assured her. "The best thing for us to do is get some sleep. One way or another, tomorrow is going to be a full day."

The phone rang before seven the next morning, rousing Nancy from an uneasy sleep. As she got up from her cot, she became aware of the shower running and saw that George's bed was empty. Bess was still sound asleep.

Nancy stumbled to the phone and picked it up. "Hello?"

"Nancy? This is Sergeant Stokes."

"What's up?" Nancy asked, instantly alert.

"No sign of Munk. That phone number in his room was a gardening supply place. A man with Munk's description bought a supply of a powerful pesticide. The active ingredient is nicotine."

"Nicotine? You mean like in tobacco?"

"Right. It's a colorless liquid alkaloid. A minute amount in a glass of water can be fatal. Munk obviously studied chemistry. The lab guys say you can distill the stuff out without sophisticated equipment."

"Oh, no," Nancy said, feeling a sense of foreboding. "Is it tasteless, too?"

"Actually, according to the lab people, it's very bitter and unpleasant."

"I can't see how he'd sneak it into anyone's food or drink, then," Nancy mused aloud.

"Me, neither. Have you come up with any brilliant ideas on how we can grab Munk?"

"I'm afraid not," Nancy said glumly.

Sergeant Stokes was silent for a moment. "Neither have we," he said. "We're going to let Annette run. Our only hope is to draw him out that way."

"What's the plan?" Nancy asked.

"Zandt and I are going to be just behind the starting area by eight. That's where to find us, if you need us. We've got all the officers we can to work the marathon. They'll be strung along the course, in radio contact with us. And we've got a guy on a scooter, but I'm not sure how much good he'll be able to do. We've got strict orders from the runners association not to interfere with the top runners' progress."

After thanking the sergeant, Nancy hung up. She quickly dressed in jeans and a shirt.

"Breakfast time," George announced brightly, emerging from the bathroom. She was wrapped in one of the hotel's huge, fluffy bath towels and was drying her hair with another.

Nancy gave her Stokes's news. "I don't get it. What will Munk do with nicotine?" George asked.

Nancy shrugged. "Maybe try to poison Annette with it, though I have no idea how," she admitted.

"Ugh!" said George, shivering. "I'm glad the cops are going to be protecting her." Patting her stomach, she said, "I'm going to burn a lot of fuel today. I need breakfast. I can be ready in five minutes. What about you guys?"

"I'll be ready," Nancy said. "But I don't know about Bess." As Nancy headed into the bathroom, she called loudly, "Bess! Wake up!"

"Mmmph," muttered Bess, opening one eye.

"I heard, I heard. I'll meet you in the coffee shop in about twenty minutes, okay?"

"Okay, but get a move on," said George, who was putting on silky blue shorts and her Heartland Marathon T-shirt with her race number, 6592, pinned to it.

A few minutes later George and Nancy were sitting in the coffee shop. They ordered, and as soon as their breakfast was served, George dug into her huge plate of pancakes with gusto.

"You need carbohydrates when you're going to be burning energy at the rate I will be today."

"I know, I know," Nancy said, laughing. "You've told us often enough." Nancy did not feel hungry, though, and barely touched her bacon and eggs. Through the coffee shop's glass wall, she watched the buzzing activity in the lobby.

"Who are all those people?" she asked George, pointing to a large group, all of whom were wearing orange Day-Glo vests with H_2O marked on the backs in big block letters.

"They're the volunteers who'll be manning the water stations," George explained. "The stations are at intervals along the course. The volunteers hand out water and sports drinks as we go by. You get pretty dehydrated, you know."

"I'll bet," Nancy said. "Running twenty-six miles must—" She broke off and stared into the lobby. "George, look."

A middle-aged man had just staggered in through the front door, bleeding from a gash on his forehead. He was quickly helped to a chair by a couple of the volunteers.

"Come on," Nancy said, getting up from the table. "I want to see what this is about."

"He just sprang at me," the man was saying when Nancy and George reached him. "Hit me with a tire iron, yanked off my vest, and ran."

"You mean the H_2O vest?" Nancy asked.

The man nodded just as the hotel's doctor arrived. Nancy stepped back to give the doctor room.

"George, that's it!" Nancy said excitedly, grabbing George's arm. "Munk is going to be at one of those stations with his own supply of doctored water. That's how he'll try to poison Annette!"

George stared at her in horror.

"The worst thing is," Nancy went on grimly, "there are dozens of stations. We don't have a clue as to which one he'll be at!"

Chapter

Eighteen

THIS IS AWFUL!" George exclaimed. "What can we do?"

"I'm not sure," said Nancy. "Let's finish breakfast and talk."

Back at the table George stared glumly down at her stack of cold pancakes.

"How do the water stations work?" Nancy asked.

"They have cups on a table, and the volunteers fill them from big containers. Then they hold the cups out to runners as they go by." George shot Nancy a worried glance. "You think Munk will try to slip Annette a cup of bad water?"

"Probably," Nancy replied. "She'll be concentrating on the race. There's a good chance she'll grab the water without looking at him."

"Hi, guys!" Bess said brightly. She sat down at the table and opened a menu. "Any news on Munk?" When Nancy explained about the nicotine, Bess looked appalled.

"I was wondering how anyone would drink the stuff if it tastes so bad," Nancy went on. "But when you're dehydrated, you'd gulp it down before you realized what it was. By then it's too late."

George jumped up from the table. "We'd better tell the police what's going on, right now!"

The starting area at Daley Plaza was total bedlam when the charter bus from the hotel let off Nancy, Bess, George, and dozens of other runners. Runners swarmed all over, doing stretches, jogging in place, and finding their starting positions behind the red ribbon strung across a street bordering the plaza.

"The top runners have their own starting point a few blocks away," George explained. "That way their start isn't hampered by the pack—that's regular runners like me."

"I hope the police already have a man with Annette," Nancy said. "Oh—there they are." She pointed to a patrol car parked about fifty yards away. Sergeant Stokes and Detective Zandt were standing next to it.

"I'd better join the runners," George said, bouncing up and down on the balls of her feet. Nancy could see that despite the danger, George was really excited about this marathon.

"Good luck," she said, hugging George. "I know you'll do great. And look at the volunteers before you drink any water—and take just a tiny taste first. Then spit it out if it tastes bad!"

"I will. I hope you find Munk before anyone else gets hurt," George said.

Bess suddenly grinned, pointing over George's shoulder. "Look who's here!" she said.

Kevin Davis, wearing a maroon ICT blazer, was making his way through the crowd toward them. Behind him, near the starting line, Nancy saw an ICT van with a cameraman perched on top, getting shots of the vast sea of runners.

George's eyes sparkled as she turned and saw Kevin. "Hi!" she said.

"I can't stay," Kevin said, fingering the silver charm around George's neck. "See you at the finish line, George," he said, gently squeezing her shoulder. "Good luck."

As George went off to join the growing mob of entrants, an idea suddenly occurred to Nancy. Turning to Kevin, she said, "I need your help."

"Now? I'm pretty busy, Nancy. Can't it wait?"

"This is a matter of life and death," Nancy replied. "I mean that literally."

Kevin frowned, but he let Nancy lead him over to Sergeant Stokes and Detective Zandt.

"We found out something that might help find him," Nancy said. She told the officers about the man they suspected was Munk stealing a Day-Glo vest from a water volunteer.

Detective Zandt listened while leaning against the door of the police car. "Let's have the men pay special attention to those water stations," he told his partner.

Sergeant Stokes nodded and gave orders on the squad car radio.

"How can *I* help?" Kevin asked.

"You'll be following the lead runners, right?" Nancy asked. When he nodded, she said, "I want to ride with your van, along with Sergeant Stokes or Detective Zandt. That way we can grab Munk when he makes his move."

Kevin looked dubious. "I don't know. We're crowded as it is," he explained. "There's the cameraman, a sound man, and the driver and me, plus racks of gear . . ."

His voice trailed off as he saw the determined expression on Nancy's face. "Oh, all right," he relented. "I guess I can fit you in."

"Good," Stokes said. "I'll stay here, since this is our central communications base. Zandt, you and Nancy and her friend go with the ICT van. Take a radio and stay in touch."

"Let's go," the detective said.

Nancy, Bess, and the detective followed as Kevin sprinted toward his van, dodging through the crowd. Within five minutes they were all set up. Kevin and his crew manned the van's rooftop camera, and Zandt, Nancy, and Bess sat below. At the detective's request the van's rear doors were tied open, so they would have the clearest view possible of the runners and the water stations.

"I don't think Munk will make a move until the middle of the race," said Nancy as they drove to the other starting line. "He'd want to catch

Annette when she's likely to be tired and dehydrated and really in need of that drink."

The detective nodded, his eyes on the runners. "I hope we'll be able to keep track of Annette in this crowd."

Following his gaze, Nancy spotted Annette and Renee in the prime spots at the starting line. Dozens of runners stood crowded together behind them. "They won't stay all jammed together for long," Nancy said. "They'll thin out."

A voice over a loudspeaker said, "The Heartland Marathon will begin in one minute."

There was electricity in the air. Runners and technicians stood waiting. "Take your marks," said the amplified voice. "Get set . . ."

The sound of the starter's gun made Nancy jump. The next thing she knew, the top runners were setting off. The van moved forward at roughly the runners' pace, and Nancy, Bess, and Detective Zandt craned their necks to keep Annette in view. Above them the cameraman was getting panoramic shots of the runners as they jockeyed for position. Kevin was speaking into a microphone.

As Nancy had predicted, it wasn't long before some runners moved ahead. Annette established herself as the front runner, slightly ahead of Renee. The crowds lining the route cheered the runners as they passed.

As the van reached the first water station, Nancy tried to focus on each volunteer in turn. There was no sign of Munk. At each succeeding station she felt more tense, wondering, Could this be the one?

At the twelve-mile mark they hadn't seen Munk yet. They passed the halfway mark at just over thirteen miles. Still nothing.

"We've been at this for over an hour," Bess said, her eyes scouring the crowds lining the course.

"Water station up ahead on our right," Detective Zandt called.

Nancy watched closely. The large folding table held many cups and was manned by a dozen or so volunteers. The van was ten yards ahead of Annette when Nancy saw a volunteer with longish dark hair edge forward with two paper cups in his hand. She stared to make absolutely certain . . .

"It's him!" she said, keeping her voice down so that Munk wouldn't hear. "In front of the table!"

At a word from Detective Zandt the van slowed to a crawl, and he, Nancy, and Bess jumped out. "Stokes? We have him spotted," Detective Zandt said into his radio as he went. He quickly gave the location.

Nancy hit the ground running and dashed toward Munk. She was ten yards away when he saw her. For an instant his eyes locked with hers. Then he whirled and started to sprint away.

Nancy was on him before he could get up any speed. She launched herself forward, slamming her shoulder into his legs, and he crumpled forward. Before he could get up, Detective Zandt had pinioned Munk's hands behind his back and put handcuffs on him. He jerked the man roughly to his feet.

"Are you crazy?" Munk shouted. "I'm a volunteer here!"

"It's all over," Nancy told him. "We know everything . . . Mr. Munk. When Gina Giraldi recovers, she'll be able to put you away for a long time."

Calvin Munk paled, and his jaw muscles clenched. "I should have killed her when I had the chance!" he spat out. "And Annette—she deserves to die! She ruined my life! She remembered me . . . the scandal. She threatened to go public—"

"Don't worry," Bess cut in. "Annette will pay for what she did, too."

While the detective read Munk his rights, two squad cars pulled up on a side road, sirens wailing.

"Why did you attack Gina Giraldi?" Nancy asked as two uniformed officers came to take Calvin Munk away. "Did she recognize you, too?"

The man nodded. "I think so. I recognized *her,* from Europe. When I heard that reporter say that Gina would expose someone connected with the marathon, I couldn't take the chance that it was me. I had to shut her up first."

"*You* were the one who tried to drop that huge pot on our heads!" Bess accused.

Munk glared at her. "You were stupid not to get the message and back off." He was still ranting angrily when the patrolmen led him to their car.

"Come on," Detective Zandt said, heading for the other squad car.

"Where are we going?" Nancy asked.

"To the finish line," he replied. "You want to

be there when we collar Annette Lang, don't you?"

The finish line was in Grant Park, under a decorative archway. A digital clock on top of the arch ticked off the time elapsed since the start of the race. It read 2:18. Reporters, photographers, and fans were waiting for the lead runners to appear.

Nancy noticed Irene Neff pacing nervously near the red tape. She went over to the woman and told her about Calvin Munk. Irene's jaw dropped in amazement.

"Renee will be upset," she said. "Charles helped to make her what she is."

Nancy returned to where Bess, Detective Zandt, and Sergeant Stokes were standing, just beyond the reporters at the finish line.

"The lead runners will be here in about fifteen minutes," Sergeant Stokes informed them. "Last we heard, Renee Clark and Annette Lang were neck and neck."

"I wonder how George is doing?" said Bess.

"She won't finish for at least an hour after the winner," Nancy said.

Soon she heard a burst of cheering and applause, then more cheering, even closer. As the cheering grew still louder, she saw Renee Clark sprint to the tape. She looked tired and winded, but her face was lit up in a winner's smile. Behind her by a hundred yards was Annette Lang, running as hard as she could.

Irene Neff rushed up to Renee, and the two

hugged. Nancy heard Renee ask, "Where's Charles?"

"He couldn't be here," said Irene. "I'll explain after you meet the press." Renee's beaming grin faded to a look of puzzled concern, but she let herself be led to the circle of reporters.

As Annette crossed the finish line, cameras flashed, and there was more cheering. The detectives waited until she had caught her breath, then approached her.

"We'd like to talk to you, Ms. Lang," said Sergeant Stokes.

"Now? Why?" Annette asked, taken aback. "It'll have to wait—I'll be with the press for a while."

"Do you want your arrest filmed for the evening news?" Stokes asked.

Annette gave a short, sharp laugh. "My *arrest?* I'm the victim here, remember?"

"Annette, I found out who was responsible for the threats against you," Nancy said, meeting Annette's glare. "I found out that it was you."

"Calvin Munk is under arrest," Sergeant Stokes added. "He's talking to my men now."

When Annette didn't say anything, Nancy said, "That's a nasty bruise on your shin. That must be from when I kicked you, after you attacked me at the Winning Margin."

Annette gave a long sigh, "You could never understand," she said. "After all this time in the spotlight, I couldn't see myself becoming a has-been, tomorrow's trivia. I figured if I could get a shot at TV work, I'd still be a somebody."

"How did you connect Munk and Mellor?" Nancy wanted to know.

"His handwriting," Annette said. "He looks a lot different now from the way he did then—new hair color, clean-shaven, thinner—everything. But once I saw his writing, I saw through the rest. I knew it was him."

Annette smiled, as if she were proud of her treachery. "He once sent me a note of congratulations for a race I won in France. The day we got here, I saw him pin a note to Renee on the message board, and I recognized the writing—it's very distinctive. I already had the plan, but I needed someone to help me, and I put the pressure on him. But I had nothing to do with Gina!" she exclaimed. "That was his doing!"

"You still have plenty to answer for," Sergeant Stokes said, leading her to a police car. He stopped and turned to Nancy.

"I have to hand it to you. You'd make a fine police officer."

Nancy blushed and murmured her thanks. The police drove away with Annette, but Nancy and Bess waited for George near the huge digital clock. Kevin joined them a while later.

More and more runners were coming across the finish line. A few collapsed and were helped up by volunteers and taken to first-aid stations.

"There she is!" Bess screamed, pointing down the course. It was George, looking more elated than tired. At the finish line she looked up at the clock, and her face lit up.

Bess rushed over and flung her arms around her. "Three hours, forty-seven minutes! A per-

148

sonal record!" George gasped, returning Bess's hug and then doing the same with Nancy. "Munk," she said, "is he—"

"In custody. Annette, too," Nancy assured her.

"Hi," said Kevin, giving George a big hug. "Good work. I was thinking of making a trip to River Heights—maybe in a week," Kevin went on. "How does that sound?"

"It sounds perfect," George told him, grinning. "I can't wait!"

Kevin turned to Bess. "Listen, I have a friend I think you'd like to meet. Want me to call him tonight? We can all go out to dinner together."

Bess's blue eyes shone for a second. Then she got a suspicious look on her face.

"What does he do?"

"He's a runner, middle-distance events—"

"No, thanks," Bess said, cutting him off. "I'll pass."

"But why?" Kevin asked, perplexed.

"I've sworn off runners," she said. "They all have one-track minds—and the only thing on them is track!"

Nancy's next case:

George's boyfriend, sportscaster Kevin Davis, is covering the National Figure Skating Championships in Chicago, and he's asked Nancy and George along to watch the show. But the action on the ice quickly sends a chill through the crowd. A top woman skater takes a terrible fall, sending her to the hospital in critical condition —and Nancy suspects sabotage!

There's more at stake than a chance to compete in the World Championships in Berlin. The top-secret computer chips in the arena's state-of-the-art scoreboard have vanished and may be headed for foreign shores, as well. Nancy, meanwhile, is headed for a dance with danger in a slippery world of fierce competition, ambition, and industrial espionage . . . in *CUTTING EDGE*, Case #70 in the Nancy Drew Files™.

Forthcoming titles in the Nancy Drew Files ™ Series